Disclaimer:

This is a work of fiction. Names, characters, businesses, places, events, locales, and incidents are either the products of the author's imagination or used in a fictitious manner. Any resemblance to actual persons, living or dead, or actual events is purely coincidental.

For Christine

"Of our dear father, and even of our only loved one, we — knowing everything — in fact, know nothing at all."
Yevgeny Yevtushenko

Contents

Chapter One (the Ks)

A Slight Turbulence

It all came – quite literally – out of the blue and cloudless sky behind the plane windows.

"Ladies and gentlemen, please fasten your seat belts: we are entering an area of slight turbulence!"

The voice of the captain on the intercom was cheerful, almost triumphant – as if he had just won a EuroMillions jackpot.

"They probably take a special crash course in how to make optimistic announcements when the plane is about to crash," Viktor whispered to his wife Katherine, sitting next to him. He smiled at his own unintended pun.

"Not a good time to talk about crashes," she remarked, sticking the end of her seat belt into the socket until it clicked.

"Come on, Kat! It is just a slight turbulence!" said Viktor, with an emphasis on "slight".

"They always say 'slight' turbulence," his wife retorted. "Have you ever heard them call turbulence anything but 'slight'?"

Viktor and Katherine Petroff were returning from a short holiday in Majorca. It had been a tradition with the Petroffs to take a weekend or so off every two or three months, rather than embarking on a two-week-long beach or cruising holiday once a year and using almost all of their modest leave allocations in one go. Another reason for taking several shorter holidays rather than a long one was Sharik, their beloved black poodle, who did not like being left in the company of Katherine's mother for more than a few days, after which he would grow uncharacteristically quiet, as if indeed depressed, and would spend his days sitting on the patio and howling almost non-stop.

Normally, the Petroffs would fly somewhere warm and seaside-ish: Italy, South of France, Greece or Turkey. But on that occasion they chose the Balearics, or Majorca to be more precise – the island that always had a special attraction for Katherine since her parents used to take her there often as a little girl. As for Viktor, whose roots were in the Russian North, the island, with its mild subtropical climate and warm sea, represented a suppressed childhood dream of a paradise on earth, the dream that had finally come true…

The Petroffs had had a relaxing long weekend in Port de Pollenca, with Katherine relaxing on the beach while Viktor, who hated swimming and sunbathing, read a book on their hotel room balcony facing the sea. Or took a bus to the ancient town of Alcudia where a spectacular Roman amphitheatre was being dug out by archaeologists. They would then meet up for lunch or dinner at one of the countless tapas restaurants lining the promenade. Five full days of such unhurried lifestyle were usually enough to relax them completely and make them forget about their UK routine, with Viktor working as a copywriter at a small advertising agency in the town where they lived, and Katherine commuting to London where she was a receptionist at the Moorfields Eye Hospital.

It all went well until that fateful lunch in a small seafood restaurant in Palma where they stopped on the way to the airport to catch an evening flight back home. Katherine got severe food poisoning from either prawns, or possibly scallops – they never found out. Minutes after the meal, she felt excruciatingly painful stomach cramps, followed by violent projectile vomiting. So severe were the symptoms that the Petroffs had to cancel their return flight and let Katherine recover first. They booked three nights at the lovely BonSol hotel in the outskirts of the city. The hotel had cosy air-conditioned rooms and its own little beach. After three days and nights of dieting and procrastination, Katherine was strong enough to travel again. In fact, she felt better that ever – rested and relaxed after that unexpected round of intensive body cleansing.

Halfway into their newly booked return flight to London Stansted, the captain announced an approaching "slight turbulence" and advised the passengers to fasten their seat belts.

The Boeing was tossed about in the sky like a lump of ice in a cocktail mixing glass of that mighty bartender called God. Some bags and suitcases fell out of overhead lockers, which sprang open like flick-knife blades, and down onto the passengers' heads. Women were screaming...

Then it all suddenly stopped. The plane straightened up its course, and was floating smoothly through the deep-blue sky, interspersed with occasional tiny clouds...

"Thank God, it's over," Katherine said to her husband. "That 'slight' turbulence was so bad I thought I was going to die there and then... I even started to compose a farewell note in my mind..."

"Yeah... it was quite scary!" agreed Viktor. It was a rare acknowledgement for a political defector from the former USSR who had gone through lots of truly turbulent stuff in his life.

"Or maybe we were destined to miss our original flight, Vitya?" his wife carried on. "Maybe we have died and are now in an afterlife of sorts?"

"Katya, please calm down. It is all over: no more turbulence – slight or severe. And, as they assured us repeatedly at my Soviet university, the afterlife doesn't exist. We had a special subject – 'scientific atheism', compulsory for all, and one of its cornerstones was that the afterlife is a myth!"

"A myth? But isn't the Soviet Union itself now part of it too, the prolonged afterlife myth I mean?"

"Let's not argue about it, Katya. We are about to start descending anyway. Look around: the same passengers who boarded the plane with us in Palma, and none of them seems to be panicking. I do admire your fellow countrymen for that amazing quality of theirs – staying cool under any circumstances. So take a deep breath and get ready for landing, my darling."

Soon the plane, having hopped over the English Channel, slowly, as if reluctantly, began its descent. Ten minutes later it touched the ground and after a couple of bounces was taxiing along the tarmac towards the airport building.

Viktor looked out of the window. It was still light, yet the huge neon sign "STANSTEAD" on the roof of the glass-and-concrete terminal was already lit up, with all its nine giant letters blinking in the dusk.

"They may be able to stay calm, your compatriots, but they certainly don't know how to spell," remarked Viktor. "Isn't it bizarre that my colleagues always ask me, a foreigner, to do a final proof of their copy?"

"What do you mean?" asked his wife.

"Here, have a look!" Viktor moved away from the window. "I always thought that the word 'Stansted' had only eight letters, with the penultimate one being 'e' not 'a', although many would be inclined to spell it as 'stead' – like in 'Hampstead', or 'homestead', say…"

"Don't be so boring, Vitya," his wife shrugged. "It is probably just a typo."

"A typo? On an airport sign? You must be joking, sweetheart! Had one of the letters been missing, that could have been easier to explain – it could have just fallen off. Once when I landed in Sophia, the capital of Bulgaria, I was amused to see that the letters on the airport roof said 'SOFA'. But that was post-communist Bulgaria in the mid-1990s in the grips of political turmoil and general neglect. In fact, 'SOFA' sounded rather comforting as a place for landing… he-he… But here we have an EXTRA letter 'a' which can be explained by just one word – 'illiteracy'!"

Viktor kept fuming all the way to passport control where he had to calm down, still not quite used to brandishing his new British passport which he had received several months earlier, after many years of waiting.

The second surprise was awaiting the Petroffs in the long-stay car park where they had left their old Volvo. The car was simply not there – neither in Zone C, row ten straight under the lantern, nor anywhere else. Even more surprisingly, on the very spot they had left the car there was another Volvo, looking like a twin of their own – same make, same beige colour, but with different number plates! Almost the same as theirs, 'T787 HEX', yet with one different letter – 'T787 HAX'.

On a more thorough inspection, the Petroffs decided that the car must have been theirs, after all: Katherine's old tartan umbrella, bought during a rainy weekend break in Edinburgh, was on the back seat, next to Viktor's denim baseball cap. Katherine hated that cap saying that it made Viktor look like a typical East European builder, to which her husband would normally respond: "But this is a compliment, darling! They are all muscular handsome guys brilliant in DIY, whereas my hands grow from the wrong place, as my late mum used to say."

Indeed, his hand was trembling a little as he inserted the key in the slot. The doors opened with a loud pop of the central lock.

"Bloody hooligans! Why did they choose to repaint that one letter? Don't they guard this car park at all? It is like having a flat tyre... worse even..."

At least the traffic was still on the right – left side of the road here, the fact that calmed Viktor down somewhat.

Halfway home, the motorway was blocked by police cars with blinking lights. "Divercion!" said an impromptu yellow road sign, with an arrow pointing left.

"Damn it!" Viktor swore. "It will take us an additional half hour to reach home now. And look: another spelling mistake, this time on the sign. I always thought that this country's cops were no great intellectuals in the main."

"You sound like a snob, Vitya," his wife replied. "The sign must have been written in a hurry. They probably had to deal with a serious road accident in which people may have been injured or even died, and here you are: sitting in your car fit as a fiddle and nit-picking!"

Viktor shrugged and turned the wheel sharply left to follow the diversion. As they were leaving the accident scene, Katherine looked right and saw a badly damaged car covered with a tarpaulin cloth. Despite its nearly flattened bumper and bent roof, she couldn't help noticing that it was the same colour and, most probably, the same make as their own vintage Volvo.

"Wait!" Katherine yelled as Viktor was backing the car into the drive in front of their cottage.

"What now?" her husband breathed out angrily as he pressed down the brake pedal.

"There is someone inside the house!" Katherine whispered. "The lights are on and I've just seen a shadow move behind the kitchen curtain… Oh, my God. We are being burgled!"

Viktor craned his neck and looked back from behind the wheel.

"You are right, Katya! I saw a shadow too."

Gently, he steered the car out of the drive and back into the dark street. He parked across the road from their cottage, under a tree. From there, the Petroffs had a good view of the house. The lights were indeed burning brightly on both floors. They could suddenly hear very clearly the muffled signature tune of the BBC TV News.

"Bloody cheek!" exclaimed Viktor. "Not only have they broken into our property, they are watching our telly too!"

"They probably know that we are away on holiday and think they are perfectly safe to do what they want," his wife agreed.

"No more talking. Let's call the police!" Viktor was already clutching his mobile.

"Damn it!" he swore after a moment. "I dial 999, and it says the number is not recognised!"

"Are you dialling carefully? Your hands must be shaking from the shock, Vitya. Let me redial."

Kat took the phone, but didn't have time to dial. The side kitchen door of the cottage sprang open. Out came a man in a tracksuit and slippers. He was moving slowly, with a slight limp, as if in pain. In his hand he was holding a plastic bag filled with rubbish. Having shuffled heavily along the gravel towards one of the three rubbish bins near the fence, he chose the brown one, opened the lid and tossed the bag inside.

"Don't forget the papers!" a woman's voice called out from inside the cottage.

The man stumbled back towards the kitchen door, went inside – and in a minute or so re-emerged with a stack of newspapers which – with obvious relief – he lowered into a plastic crate, next to the rubbish bin. Having done that, he trudged back inside and locked the door behind him.

The Petroffs were speechless.

"Can you pinch me, Katya?" said Viktor. "Did you see what I saw? Or have I gone totally crazy under Majorca's burning sun? Troppo, as they say in Australia."

"I saw it too!" his wife whispered back. "A burglar considerate enough to take out the rubbish from the house he just raided."

"He has an accomplice!" continued Viktor. "A woman judging by the voice. Or another man with a high-pitch feminine voice... you never know these days."

"The man didn't look like a criminal," Katherine went on. "In fact, he looked rather harmless, even pitiful, with that heavy limp of his. He also... he also... no, that couldn't be..."

She fell silent.

"What did you want to say? He was also what? Finish your sentence!" demanded Viktor.

"Well, if you insist... but you are not going to like it... He looked like a spitting image of yourself, Vitya!"

"What? You must be hallucinating, darling!"

"No, I am not. He looked very much like your non-existent twin brother. Maybe that was because he was wearing your domestic tracksuit and your slippers?"

"Was he? I thought those did look familiar. Listen, Katya. You stay in the car, but I am going there to have a showdown with these guys, no matter who they are!"

"Don't Vitya. They may be armed!"

"I don't think so. If the man was indeed my lookalike, I can't imagine him... me... with a gun, and you yourself said he looked harmless..."

"Yes, but his accomplice could be different," Katherine objected meekly.

"The one with the high-pitched voice? I don't think so."

Viktor got out of the car and paced resolutely towards the cottage.

His wife dashed after him. "Vitya, wait! Take this!" she handed him her old tartan umbrella. "Just in case. At least you'll have something to protect yourself if they attack you. And please don't use our keys to open the door: you may surprise them and make them do something unpredictable. It's safer to just knock."

Viktor took the umbrella. "Please, get back into the car," he said and knocked at the door of his own cottage – loudly and decisively.

"Open up!" he yelled. "The owners are back!"

"Vitya, someone is at the door!" a woman's voice said from inside the house. Anxious as Viktor was, he could hear each word very clearly. The strangest thing was that the voice sounded precisely like that of his wife, Katherine.

Chapter Two (the Cs)

A Gentle Collision

It all came – quite literally – out of the blue. It was a beautiful
summer afternoon – one of those scorching days, rare even for the
South of England, when the merciless red-hot disc of the sun, with a
couple of small puffy clouds around it, resembled a portion of bacon
and eggs on the azure frying pan of the sky. The air bursting from the
rolled down car window (the old Volvo had no air-conditioning) was
thick and hazy. It was hitting Victor's face, as if his right cheek was
being repeatedly slapped with a hot wet rag, each time momentarily
blocking his vision.

Having landed at Stansted airport an hour earlier, Victor Petrov
and his wife Catherine were on their way home after a short holiday
in Majorca. It had been a tradition with the Petrovs to take a
weekend or so off every two or three months, rather than embarking
on a two-week-long beach or cruising holiday once a year and using
almost all of their modest leave allocations in one go. Another reason
for taking several shorter holidays rather than a long one was Sharik,
their beloved white poodle, who did not like being left in the
company of Catherine's father for more than a few days, after which
he would grow uncharacteristically quiet, as if indeed depressed, and
would spend his days sitting on the patio and howling almost non-
stop.

Normally, the Petrovs would fly somewhere warm and seaside-ish:
Italy, South of France, Greece or Turkey. But on that occasion they
chose the Balearics, or Majorca to be more precise – the island that
always had a special attraction for Catherine since her parents used to
take her there as a little girl. As for Victor, whose roots were in
Central Russia, the island, with its mild subtropical climate and warm

sea, represented a suppressed childhood dream of a paradise on earth, the dream that had finally come true…

The Petrovs had had a relaxing long weekend in Pollenca, with Victor sunbathing on the beach in between frequent dips into the emerald, but still cold, sea and brisk, yet powerful, swims to the buoy and back to the shore. Victor would turn up on the beach daily – just to lie in the sun, while Catherine read on the balcony, or took a bus to the ancient town of Alcudia where a spectacular Roman amphitheatre was being dug out by archaeologists. They would then meet up for lunch or dinner at one of the countless tapas restaurants lining the promenade. Five full days of such unhurried lifestyle were usually enough to relax them completely and make them forget about their UK routine, with Victor working as editor of a small technology magazine, whose editorial offices were based in the town where they lived, and Catherine commuting to London by train and then taking the Tube to Hampstead where she worked as a medical secretary to a cardiac surgeon at the Royal Free Hospital near Belsize Park Tube station.

As they were spending their final day of holidays in the island's capital, Palma, they decided to visit the beach for the last time before flying back.

This time, Victor's usual far-from-the-shore swim ended badly: his right hand was rather painfully stung by a Portuguese Man of War jellyfish, hiding underneath the buoy, which Victor slapped inadvertently, or rather somewhat ostentatiously, for his wife on the shore to see: look how far away I am. It felt as if a sharp razor blade cut through the back of his palm. Catherine, who hated swimming and sunbathing, could hear him cry out in pain from the beach where she was sitting in the shade immersed in a book. They had to visit a pharmacy and buy a special anti-sting ointment, which did not stop Victor's stung hand from swelling.

The swelling was getting worse by the minute. It looked precarious and was painful to the touch. Victor was also feeling feverish – not up for flying, so the Petrovs had to cancel their return flight and let Victor recover first. They booked three nights at a two-star Horizonte hotel in the suburb of Iletas – just fifteen minutes by bus from the city centre. The hotel had cosy air-conditioned rooms, with calming views of the bay. After three days and nights of intense treatment, the swelling on Victor's hand disappeared, and he was strong enough to travel again. In fact, he felt better than ever – rested and relaxed after that unexpected spell of enforced procrastination.

Halfway into their newly booked return flight to London Stansted, the captain announced an approaching "slight turbulence" and advised the passengers to fasten their seat belts.

The Boeing was tossed about in the sky like a lump of ice in a cocktail mixing glass of that mighty bartender called God. Some bags and suitcases fell out of overhead lockers, which sprang open like flick-knife blades, and down onto the passengers' heads. Women were screaming…

Then it all suddenly stopped. The plane straightened up its course, and was floating smoothly through the deep-blue sky, interspersed with occasional tiny clouds.

They landed in Stansted without incident, found their old Volvo in the long-term car park and set off on a 40-minute-long drive back home.

Neither Catherine, dozing off in the passenger seat, nor Victor struggling not to succumb to drowsiness behind the wheel, could see the green Mini around a sharp bend in the road – and when they did, it was already too late. The little green car was probably overtaking another vehicle, or had simply lost direction, for otherwise why on earth did it suddenly find itself on the wrong side of the road straight in front of the Petrovs' old Volvo, so close that Victor didn't have any time left to swerve?

Catherine shut her eyes. "This is it!" was the only thought that flashed through her mind as the two cars collided – head on.

The impact was both strong and blunt, like a sudden pang of dull stomach ache. The belated screeching of brakes, the grinding of bent metal and the rustling of disintegrating glass – all merged into an ear-grating cacophony which lasted both forever and for just a fraction of a second, or so it felt. Victor was thrown forward, towards the windscreen, and immediately felt a sharp pain in his ribs. At least the seat belt stopped him from hitting the windscreen glass – or what remained of it – with his head.

He had a momentary blackout, and when he came to – he was stunned, almost deafened, by the sudden eerie silence. The only sounds he was aware of were peaceful: an almost matter-of-fact chirping of crickets in the dusty roadside grass and the whisper-like soft rustles of the engine oil dripping ever so slowly and strangely calmingly – drip, drip, drip – from the smashed oil tank onto the ground.

"Are... you... ok?" Catherine's feeble voice sounded from the passenger seat.

Victor opened his eyes and – with an effort – turned his head slightly to the left. Catherine's face was pale, with a small trickle of blood oozing from a nostril.

"Fine. And you?"

"Don't know, Vitya. It was all so sudden... Not sure if I am still alive or dead. Maybe we were destined to miss our original return flight, to die in a car crash on the way home and are now in an afterlife of sorts?"

"We'll be ok, Katya, and the afterlife doesn't exist, don't you know that?" Victor chuckled. It was not a proper care-free dry chuckle, but rather an attempt at one which sounded more like a cough than a cackle.

"We are still talking to each other which can mean only one thing – we ARE alive! Not so sure about the guys in the Mini though," he said.

The Petrovs' old Volvo, whose battered body was lined with powerful steel bars, was indeed remarkably unscathed, not counting a large dent on the right side of the bonnet, broken windows and the door on the driver's side which had got stuck on the impact and refused to open, so to get out of the car Victor had to climb over his wife and use the door on her side.

The little green Mini was thrown off the road and was now resting on its roof in the ditch. As Victor made several unsteady steps towards it – intending to check on its driver and passengers, if any – a teenage boy, no older than fifteen, climbed from under the overturned car and started running away from it, as if expecting the Mini to explode. He was obviously in a shock, for having run no more than fifty yards, he halted abruptly and collapsed onto the ground. As Victor was watching the boy, a teenage girl, of about the same age, emerged from under the wreckage and was now sitting on the ground staring in front of her with glassy unseeing eyes.

"Thank God, they are both alive," Victor thought. In the distance, he could hear a siren and soon saw the blinking blue lights of an approaching police car. Or possibly an ambulance.

"You guys must thank your lucky stars!" a young paramedic was telling the Petrovs inside the ambulance which was taking them home. Having checked them thoroughly, he found no serious trauma – just a couple of fractured ribs between the two of them – a common consequence of a whiplash. Victor could taste blood in his mouth. He had lost a front tooth, which had been wobbly for some time anyway. Catherine had a lump on the bridge of her nose and a bruise on her right knee where it had hit the gear stick. The kids from the Mini were more or less fine too. They were joy-riders of course: underage, not insured. The boy was trying to impress his girlfriend by taking her for a ride in his mum's car of which he had promptly lost control.

"A typical scenario," the paramedic was saying.

He explained how lucky the Petrovs were to be driving an old Volvo, famous for its sturdiness. Had it been a Ford Fiesta, or even a Toyota, the impact could have been different.

They had to leave the car at the site of the accident, after a quick interview with two traffic policemen who were now questioning the shocked teenage couple.

"The moment we are finished with your vehicle, we'll have it returned to your home address," one of the policemen assured the Petrovs before they were driven off.

"Do take it easy for a couple of days," advised the paramedic, having helped Victor and Catherine to carry their suitcases to the door of their cottage. "And do not forget how lucky you are. Trust me: it was a very gentle collision indeed!"

From their kitchen window, the Petrovs watched the standard red-and-black paramedics' van do a U-turn in their street and drive away slowly. They stared out of the window until they could no longer see the word "AMBULENCE" painted in large yellow letters across the van's back.

Chapter Three (the CKs)

A Double Encounter

"Vitya, will you open the door? I can hardly move!" Catherine shouted from the upstairs master bedroom.

"I will, I will… Although I am not in my best shape either," replied her husband as he limped towards the front door, which was being pounded upon in a rather aggressive manner.

"Open up! The owner is back!" a man's voice was yelling from outside.

"It is probably our police friend from the accident spot," Victor thought as he slowly turned the knob of the door lock. Each movement of his fingers resonated with a sharp pain in his torso. "He is saying that the Volvo is back, or so it sounds."

To be on the safe side, however, he decided to keep the door chain-locked for the time being.

The first thing Victor could see when the slit appeared was indeed their good old Volvo. Only it was parked not in their driveway but on the opposite side of the street, under the lime tree. Despite the darkness, he recognised it straight away: the early 1990s Volvo GLTs were rare in 2017's England. "So the late visitor must indeed be a policeman," he thought. "It is unfortunate they have the habit of pounding at every door as if there was a crime scene behind it."

Victor was about to release the chain lock, when the man outside, whom he was still unable to see, pulled the door sharply towards himself. The chain strained in its socket, keeping the door open just a tad.

"Oi! Easy, mate!" he said to the still invisible visitor. "Let go of the door – and I will then be able to open it."

What he heard in response was totally unexpected.

"Don't you tell me how to handle the door to MY house, you stupid bastard!" the man shouted in a loud and vaguely familiar voice with a distinct East European accent. "Just open the bloody door and let us in this very second. And remember: the police are on their way!"

"But... but... I thought YOU were the police," mumbled Victor.

"I wish we were! Then I could have arrested you for the break-in here and now, you dirty criminal. As it stands, I can only smash your ugly face and throw you out of my property. Or – being a civilised person – tie you up and hand you over to the police when they arrive!"

The man outside was still holding the door handle and was pulling the door towards himself whereas Victor was doing the same from the inside. The chain strained, tight as a bowstring, and the door remained semi-open (or rather semi-closed) stopping the two opposing parties from seeing each other.

"Vitya! Are you OK?" an anxious woman's voice sounded from the street. It was Katherine, who – greatly disturbed by the sounds of an argument – got out of the car and ran across the driveway into her own front garden to check on her husband. Inside the house, Victor, while still clinging to the handle, thought that his wife Catherine had left the house through the side kitchen door and was about to confront the intruder from the back – a rather foolhardy thing to do, because for all he knew, the unwanted visitor could be armed.

At this point something extraordinary happened: "Katya, keep away please!" both men shouted in unison without letting go of the handles from their respective sides of the door, their voices as matching and as synchronised as those of the Beatles in the famous "I wanna hold your hand" song refrain. In this situation, however, "I wanna hold your handle" would have been more appropriate.

The effect of that sudden synchronism was such that both men simultaneously let go of the door and fell onto their backs – Viktor onto the asphalted driveway, and Victor onto the thin corridor carpet – and whereas the former promptly jumped up and shook dust off his trousers, the latter remained supine: his ribs, damaged in the accident, resonated to the fall with sharp excruciating pain, which nearly made him faint.

From the outside – through the released door which was now wide ajar – Viktor and Katherine could see the 'burglar', dressed in Viktor's own old dressing gown, wriggling in pain on the floor, and his accomplice – a young woman in Katherine's loose 'domestic' Levis running down the stairs and screaming loudly: "Vitya, Vitya, what have they done to you?"

Prolonged silence followed.

"What the hell?" mumbled Victor after a minute or so. He stood up from the floor, staring at his opponent intently.

"Yes, what the hell is going on?" echoed his lookalike on the other side of the door.

None of the four could think of anything else to say.

It suddenly became perfectly clear to the Petroffs – as well as to the Petrovs – that, with the exception of some minor clothes and haircut details, they were facing mirror-like images of each other. And that was what they did: stared at each other without uttering a word.

"K-Katya, can you please pinch me?" Viktor said finally. "Do you see what I see?"

It was Catherine, not his wife, who responded to him from inside the cottage:

"No need to pinch anyone or anything… You just happen to be the exact copies of us…"

"I wouldn't be so sure," said Katherine from the outside. "To me at least, it is perfectly clear that it is YOU who are the copies of us, not the other way round!"

"My God, does it really matter?" interrupted Viktor. "Whoever are copies of whom, we are all like… like… monozygotic twins, which is bizarre, for I personally never had brothers or sisters, I am certain of that."

"I don't even have cousins, only second cousins," said Victor.

"And I do have a sister," said Katherine. "Only not a twin: she is four years younger than I... and prettier too."

"How interesting," exclaimed Catherine. "The only sibling I have – my brother – is exactly four years younger than I am!"

"At least, it's a brother," shrugged Katherine. "So we are not the same in everything."

"When is your sister's birthday?" Catherine asked.

"4th of April 1984."

"Oh, my: it doesn't get better, does it? My brother's birthday is on exactly the same day, same year too."

"Are you sure he wasn't born as a girl and then underwent a sex change, or gender reassignment, as we are now supposed to say?" intervened Viktor.

"It's not a good time for your silly jokes," his wife rebuffed him. "The whole thing is too serious and too baffling to be flippant about it."

"Incidentally, isn't it time to introduce ourselves to each other?" inquired Victor. "So why don't you guys come in and be our guests?"

"Thanks for inviting us into OUR own cottage!" Viktor said sarcastically.

Half an hour later, the Petroffs and the Petrovs were sitting around the kitchen table, with a kettle and tea cups on it. The tea in all four mugs remained untouched: the couples were so involved in the conversation – or rather a discussion, or even more precisely, an argument – to be bothered about the milky and increasingly lukewarm drink Catherine had made.

Unlike the tea, however, the verbal exchange around the table was rather heated.

The two couples had so far established beyond any reasonable doubt that they were very much alike, yet not quite the same. The similarities were not limited to age and appearance. The Petrovs and the Petroffs had been married for precisely the same number of years, months and days, with their wedding anniversaries both falling on the 25th of May. Both Victor and Viktor were escapees from the former Soviet Union: the former originated from Arkhangelsk in the far north of Russia where he grew up before moving to Moscow; the latter was born and bred in the Central Russian city of Ryazan and moved to the capital several years prior to his defection. They were both born on the same day and were both naturalised as British citizens in 2002 – Viktor in March and Victor in April, but it took each of them nearly five years to get their coveted British passports.

Katherine and Catherine, in their turn, were both born in the North East of England – the former in Sunderland, the latter in Durham; both came to live in London at the age of twenty-one and both moved to Hertfordshire with their husbands in 2007, when life in the capital became too expensive. Both women met their respective partners and would-be husbands via popular dating websites: Katherine via kindredsouls.co.uk and Catherine – via loveactually.com.

"As always, you've put too much milk in the tea!" Victor remarked to his wife during one of the awkward pauses in the otherwise lively and emotional (at times overly emotional) verbal exchange. "One thing I cannot come to grips with in this country is the whole white tea concept."

"Totally agree with you!" said Viktor. "They take two good things, mix them together in one cup, add some tepid water and end up with one dull and tasteless product which they then call tea!"

"Not sure about my female namesake here, but I, like most English people, cannot stand tea without milk," objected Catherine.

Katherine raised her eye-brows: "I actually do understand your husband, for despite being English through and through I still prefer black tea, European-style, believe it or not! And what do you mean by 'namesake'? As we have established already, my name starts with 'K', yours – with 'C'.

"Yes, but they sound the same, just like those of our husbands. To me, 'Viktor', with a 'k' in the middle looks more Russian and therefore more genuine than the anglicised 'Victor' with a 'c', like in my husband's case."

"Come off it, ladies," interrupted Victor. "What's in a name, as the great William Shakespeare used to say? At least, each of us has a name of his or her own. Not sure the same can be said about the house…"

"Indeed!" agreed his male counterpart. "You guys have moved into the cottage in our absence and are now claiming it is yours. How about us? We have nowhere else to go!"

"Well, as I said before, you are welcome to stay with us for a couple of days until… until…"

"Until what? This house is as much ours as it is yours, and you have no right to invite us to stay in our own property, for which we have just finished paying the mortgage – after all those years!"

"So have we… well, almost. We've got another year of repayments left…"

"You see: this house IS ours well and truly, and we don't even have to pay for it any longer!"

"Enough bickering!" said Katherine. "Let's try and see how we can resolve this difficult situation." In her capacity as a hospital receptionist she was well accustomed to solving the patients' seemingly impossible dilemmas.

"You are right, K – sorry, can I call you 'K'?" said Victor. Katherine nodded, feeling secretly pleased to have been singled out and addressed by a name, even if a one-letter one, for the first time in the so far nameless, not counting the token "darling" and "you guys", conversation.

"Yes, K is right, we must resolve the situation," repeated Victor with a smile. "But to do so, we first have to address two questions: who exactly we are, and by 'we' I mean each of the four of us; and how – if at all – we are related to each other. We simply cannot carry on without answering them."

"What do you mean who we are?" objected Viktor. "I for myself know very well who I am!"

"You are always very sure of yourself, Vitya," his wife remarked. "But don't be too sure. I personally feel very confused sitting next to my complete namesake looking like a spitting image of myself, as I am sure you are next to your male lookalike who could be your long-lost twin brother."

"Please stop referring to us in the third person, as if we are not here, or do not exist at all," said Catherine. "I can go along with your husband in saying that I have no doubt whatsoever as to who I am either – I am Catherine Petrov, born Catherine Gregory. The one and only!"

"Wait, Catherine, or shall I call you C?" the other woman stood up from her chair. "Why not, if I have just been christened K and actually quite like it? Did you just say that your maiden name is 'Gregory'? But that is MY maiden name too! What's going on here? And indeed who are we, after all?"

"I… I cannot affirm anything, "said Victor. "But I do have a little guess which I am not ready to share with you all. Not yet… And yes, you can now call me VC and my counterpart here – VK, if you wish."

It was Catherine who broke the silence.

"Don't know about you guys, but I am too tired to keep talking!" she announced and added: "With a car crash on top of it all, one thing I fancy now is sleep which should help me forget about the pain in my ribcage for an hour or so."

"You are right, darling: 'morning is wiser than night,' as they say in Russia," her husband nodded.

"It certainly is," echoed VK. "At least there's something we seem to agree upon."

"You are welcome to stay in a spare bedroom upstairs," announced Catherine. "The bed linen is fresh, and you will find some clean towels on top of the wardrobe."

"I know where I keep MY towels," replied Katherine. "And let's call a spade a spade: it is you guys who will be staying with us, not the other way around. OK, you can have our master bedroom for yourselves. But only for tonight. Just one thing I would like to know before we all go upstairs: why on earth have you moved our lounge sofa from its normal place in the middle of the room all the way to the balcony door?"

Finally, the lights went out in the Ks' (or was it Cs'?) cottage, but long after midnight muffled voices could be heard – both from the large master bedroom and from a much smaller bedroom for guests, which the Ks used to refer to as a green room, for its walls were painted faint green, and the Cs as a beige room for it was painted accordingly. The walls in the guest room, where the Ks had been accommodated for the night, were actually neither green nor beige but light-brown, but so tired and confused were Viktor and Katherine that they didn't pay much attention to the change, having automatically dismissed it as just another inexplicable discrepancy of which they had encountered a lot on that day.

"Viktor, are you asleep?"

"That's a pointless question, Katya, to which there can be just one answer – 'no'."

"You can't help being boring, Vitya, even on a day like this."

"A day like what?"

"When we seem to have lost everything we had: our car, our house. I don't even know who we are any longer."

"I'd rather ask WHAT we are. And what THEY are. I mean those creatures behind the wall."

"Creatures? Whoever they are, they look human to me. They are our complete lookalikes, after all."

"Well, I am not so sure. For all I know, they could be some kind of robots, avatars, or just figments of our own imagination. This is in the best of scenarios."

"How about the worst?"

"In the worst of scenarios, they are some very sophisticated crooks, who have learned lots of things about us and our lives, have made themselves up to look like us, and are now trying to steal not just our identities, but our property too."

"To have gone to all that trouble, they could have chosen a much richer couple than us."

"You never know with crooks, Katya."

"Look, Vitya, I have a splitting headache. Let's try and get some sleep. I am still hoping that all this is but some very vivid nightmare and we'll wake up tomorrow morning – just the two of us, and in our cottage..."

"And, hopefully, in our own bed next door... Sweet dreams, Katya."

As the Ks were talking to each other in hushed voices, in the master bedroom, Victor and Catherine were not asleep either.

"Victor, are you asleep?"

"That's a pointless question, Cat, to which there can be just one answer – 'no'."

"You can't help being boring, Vitya, even on a day like this."

"A day like what?"

"When we nearly lost our lives in the car crash, to say nothing of those cheeky intruders next door. I am not even sure if we are alive any longer."

"I am sure that we are alive, Cat. But I am not sure where exactly we are."

"How do you mean?"

"Just thinking. What if... what if... there are not four of us here, but still just two – you and me?"

"I don't understand."

"There was an article in 'Focus' magazine recently... what if you and I – as well as that man and his wife next door – are just different versions of the same two people?"

"Can you please explain?"

"In my line of work as a technology journalist, I have to follow all the latest scientific breakthroughs and discoveries, particularly those reported by our competitive publications. I suddenly remembered a recent article in 'Focus' magazine on the Multiverse Theory. Not that the theory itself is new, but the magazine was trying to sum up the newest takes on it. It was about the theoretical possibility of the existence of countless universes populated with the same, or nearly the same people, and another – again purely theoretical – possibility of stumbling from one universe into another and being confronted with your own doubles, so to speak. I wonder if that is what may have somehow happened to us, in which case we are neither relatives nor strangers, but simply two different impressions of one and the same couple!"

"This is mind-boggling, Vitya!"

"I know. Let's talk about it all tomorrow. Thankfully, we have two more days of holidays left."

"Yes. I am still hoping that all this is but some very vivid nightmare and we'll wake up tomorrow morning on our own in our cottage."

"Me too. Sweet dreams, Catia!"

"Sweet dreams!"

Chapter Four (the KCs and the PCs)

A Mournful Intrusion

For PC Sean Dawson, the day did not start well. The moment he reported for duty at 6 am, he was called upstairs to Superintendent Burgess' office. That in itself was not a good omen.

"We had a double fatality on the R6 motorway last night. A local married couple." As he spoke, the Superintendent was looking down at his desk, rather than at PC Dawson, as if feeling *a priori* guilty for what he was about to ask him.

"Do you want me to notify the next of kin, sir?" asked PC Dawson, just for the sake of asking. He already knew what answer he was going to get.

To be a death notifier was – for obvious reasons – one of a police officer's most hated duties. But somebody had to do it, of course.

"Yes, please," the Superintendent confirmed. "Take PC Hartley and tell him I have personally asked him to accompany you."

PC Dawson was familiar with police protocol which said that death notification should be delivered in person, "in clear and plain language" and by no fewer than two officers. The main reason for having two or more officers was to be able to deal adequately with a possible "negative reaction" to the gruesome news by a person or people at the receiving end. The protocol also specified that, to make the situation feel private, the officers should only deliver the news inside the receiver's "residence".

Oh, well. Superintendent Burgess' 'request' was actually an order. Having asked PC Hartley to wait in a patrol car at the station's entrance, PC Dawson got the names of the deceased from Forensics:

"Victor and Katherine Petrovas, both aged forty-one." Cause of death – "multiple internal and external wounds after a head-on motorway collision with a dump truck."

"What happened to the other involved party?" PC Dawson asked the on-duty constable.

"The driver survived almost intact," he replied. "Just a shock and a couple of broken ribs. He is in hospital now but will probably be discharged later today."

"What about the dead couple's vehicle?" PC Dawson enquired.

"A complete write off it is, their old Volvo. Smashed almost beyond recognition, despite all its famous safety features. Nothing much they could do against a ten-ton tipper. Our boys towed the wreck to a garage nearest to the crash site to examine. When they are finished, they'll dump it."

PC Dawson wrote down the deceased couple's address and went out. An old police Ford Mondeo, with PC Hartley behind the wheel, was waiting outside.

"Let's go, Josh," PC Dawson said with a deep sigh, having installed himself in the passenger seat. "As jailbirds say, the sooner you go to prison – the sooner you come out."

Before heading for the deceased couple's address, they were to stop at the county hospital morgue, where the bodies had been kept overnight, to pick up death certificates in case the next of kin would want to see them. They were also supposed to have a quick look at the corpses, just to make sure they were indeed Victor and Katherine Petrovas and not anyone else – a necessary formality which the constables would have been more than happy to avoid.

PC Dawson turned the ignition key – once, twice, three times. On the fourth turn, the engine reluctantly started. It felt as if the car was not looking forward to their mission either.

As PC Dawson and PC Hartley were driving towards the hospital, the Cs and the Ks were back at the kitchen table having a light continental breakfast of instant coffee and sliced bread from the freezer, promptly defrosted by Catherine.

"There must be some eggs in the pantry," Katherine suggested.

Catherine checked the pantry and indeed found half a dozen of eggs. "I completely forgot we had them," she shrugged.

"Well, I haven't," replied K.

To the men's consternation, it appeared as if both women were familiar with the cottage's general layout – as well as with the contents of its fridges, wardrobes, closets and cupboards.

It was then that Victor decided to share his theory of what could have happened to them all.

"It may all sound to you like a concept from the fevered imagination of a deranged philosopher, but there is solid scientific evidence of the theoretical existence of multiple universes and the way they can manifest themselves in our everyday world, at least on a quantum level," he started in a somewhat showy manner, as if enjoying the sound of his own voice.

"Wait, not so fast," said Viktor. "I am not a technology journalist, just a modest copywriter, but I certainly have an idea of what quantum is and don't quite see how it all refers to us and to our predicament…"

"I will try to explain," said VC. "You see, the weird and wonderful world of quantum mechanics reveals that things can exist in several states at the same time and that nothing can be predicted with any certainty. And just as the massive shake up at the moment of the Big Bang must have led to the breaking of symmetry and the formation of our one universe as we know it, one of the countless number of other universes, there's no reason why less powerful sudden 'shocks', like air turbulence or a car crash, cannot 'relocate' one or two people at a time to an alternative universe, where they can – theoretically at least – bump into their own doubles or exact lookalikes…"

"Wait a moment," Viktor interrupted again. "If what you are saying is true, then on crossing over into an alternative universe, we should have bumped into our doubles, who had actually been living there since their birth and felt at home. Whereas the impressions of all four of us testify to the fact that both Katherine, sorry K, and I – as well as you and your lovely wife (he sneered at Catherine, and she smiled in return) are all struggling to come to grips with multiple deviations from our familiar reality, or realities, if you wish. This means that we are all newcomers in this particular universe, and if so then where are the local Viktor and Katherine, no matter how you spell their names? In all probability, they should have been at home – inside this very cottage when you guys arrived here after your car accident last night!"

"Yes, you are right, VK," agreed Victor. "I cannot understand that either."

"But is it possible that they…" Catherine began, when the doorbell rang suddenly, and Victor limped off to answer it.

"We are not expecting anyone," Catherine said to the Ks. "Are you?"

The Ks shook their heads.

"Vitya, wait! I am coming with you, Vitya," Catherine yelled at her husband's receding back. "You never know who could be there."

Before pressing the doorbell, PC Dawson and PC Hartley had spent several minutes in the front yard examining – or rather looking in bewilderment at – an old Volvo of the same make and colour as the one the deceased couple had been driving before the crash. Yet, very much unlike the latter – a write-off waiting to be dumped, according to Forensics – this one looked totally intact and spotlessly clean (on the way from Stanstead Viktor had stopped at a road-side car wash).

"There must have been two Volvos in the family," PC Dawson suggested to his colleague.

"Yes, but now there's only one left," agreed PC Hartley, lightly patting the car on the bumper, as if it were a pet. "You haven't, by any chance, made a note of the crashed Volvo's number plate, Sean?"

"No, I haven't – was in a bit of a rush," PC Dawson replied. "In any case, let's knock on the door and see if anyone is inside the cottage."

Catherine caught up with Victor when he was already opening the door. Remembering yesterday's confrontation with his lookalike, he had made sure the chain-lock was in place – just in case.

"Don't worry, Cat, these are policemen," he said to his wife without turning back. Through the partially open door Catherine could see two burly constables in full gear. Crackling unintelligible sounds were coming from small walkie-talkies perched on their shoulders.

"I am PC Dawson, and this is my colleague PC Hartley," one of the policemen said. "Can we please come in for a minute?"

"Of course you can, officers," smiled Victor, unlocking the door.

Victor and Catherine led the way to the lounge through a small semi-dark corridor. The two policemen followed, their radios crackling as they walked.

The Ks were no longer at the breakfast table.

"We've gone upstairs and will be back with you in a moment!" Katherine shouted from the first floor.

"Yes, please! We have police here!" Catherine shouted back.

Having entered the lounge, the policemen removed their caps.

"Can we please sit down?" asked PC Dawson. Victor and Catherine nodded. They did not like the sombre expression on the policemen's faces.

"Is… is everything ok with my mother?" Catherine asked.

"Sorry, ma'am, we don't know anything about your mother," PC Hartley responded while staring at Catherine's face intently. "We are here on a different matter."

"Apologies, officer," said Victor. "My wife's mum is quite… er… elderly, in her late seventies, so we are always worried that something might have happened to her."

"No trouble, sir. I have an elderly and infirm mother myself, so I understand you completely." While speaking, PC Dawson shifted his gaze from Victor to Catherine and then back to Victor.

"How can we help you then, officers?" Catherine said after a pause. She didn't like the way the constables were staring at her – as if she were a kind of freak, or a criminal.

"We are here to… to…" started PC Dawson. He never finished the sentence.

"Before I start, can I kindly ask you two to introduce yourselves," he said.

"Sure. We are Catherine and Victor Petrov. Married, no children," Victor reported.

"Sorry, sir, could you say your names again?" asked PC Hartley.

"Catherine and Victor Petrov," repeated Victor.

"Can I have a quick word in private with my colleague?" PC Dawson said suddenly. "Something has come up, and we have to discuss it urgently and in private. We won't be long, I promise."

PC Dawson stood up from his chair and hurried out of the room and out of the cottage. PC Hartley ran after him, while the Cs stared in consternation at their quickly receding backs.

Once outside, the policemen marched across the driveway without saying a word to each other. It was only when they were out in the street, a good fifty yards away from the house, that PC Hartley stopped and turned towards his colleague.

"Are you thinking what I am thinking?" he asked.

"Yes, Sean, I probably am. These two look exactly like that dead couple in the morgue."

"So I am not going mad then. And they have the same names too!"

"The names may sound roughly the same, but be spelled differently," PC Hartley suggested meekly. "Particularly, foreign names, like Victor. Incidentally, Catherine too can be spelled in two different ways."

"Are you saying, Josh, that we have just been talking to the twin brother and sister of the deceased whose names happen to differ from those of the dead couple only in spelling and who are also married to each other?"

"Yes, that's exactly what I was trying to say. Do you have a better theory?"

"No. You must be right, Josh. Life is full of incredible coincidences. They must indeed be close relatives of the victims who had already found out about their tragic deaths and had come to the cottage to pay their respects and to grieve."

"They didn't look too upset to me though," PC Hartley remarked. "So, most probably, they have just been house-sitting the cottage while their relatives were on holidays and are still unaware of what has happened to them."

"Whatever it is, we must go back, Josh. It is not very polite to dash out of the house like we did. Particularly when we are about to break such horrible news to the couple."

"Yes, but before we go, I'd like to contact the station and check something with them."

PC Hartley tuned his radio to the police station's frequency and asked the duty officer to check the number plate of the car that was involved in the road accident with two fatalities on the R6 motorway last night. Within seconds the constable was scribbling down the number in his notepad. "Roger and out," he said to the duty officer. He then looked up at PC Dawson.

"Sean, you are not going to like it," he said. "The number plate is the same as that of the car in the cottage's driveway."

Chapter Five

A Pointless Search

As PC Dawson and PC Hartley investigated the driveway, and the Cs (Victor and Catherine Petrov), puzzled by the policemen's sudden escape, were waiting anxiously inside the cottage, the Ks (Katherine and Viktor Petroff) were upstairs, in the cottage's third bedroom doubling as an office, huddled over Katherine's iPad Mini, which she always took with her on her travels. And puzzled they were too! In fact, to say they were just 'puzzled' would be a gross understatement. They were totally dumbfounded and profoundly shocked by what they uncovered during their attempted internet search for the term 'multiverse' – the word repeatedly used by Victor to describe their possible predicament.

The Petroffs' shock had nothing to do with the 'multiverse' itself, for they had never managed to even come close to looking it up.

To begin with, to their complete consternation, when Katherine typed the word 'google' in the so far nameless search engine box, her screen did not immediately come up with the habitual multi-coloured logo, but asked: "Did you mean 'googol'?" and then came up with following definition: "Googol – the number 10 raised to the power 100 (10^{100}), written out as the numeral 1 followed by 100 zeros."

"Hmm…" Katherine was saying ponderously as she typed 'Google search engine' before pressing the enter key again.

The screen went alive with some spider-like gibberish where the only discernible bits were *"local Cartesian hyperspacejam sqrt(3)"* and *"Content-Transfer-Encoding: 8bit."*

"I can't believe my eyes, but it looks as if Google doesn't exist," she said to Viktor who was staring at the screen from behind her back with equal disbelief.

"That is impossible!" he exclaimed loudly. "More likely, the site is simply down – having a temporary problem or undergoing maintenance."

"But Google is the biggest and most reliable search giant. As far as I know, it has never experienced problems before!"

"No-one is perfect!" shrugged Viktor. "There's always the first time. The system is obviously down, so why don't you look for another search engine – there's no shortage of those on the web?"

Katherine complied and after several minutes of feverish typing came up with *wwl.infinity.mon*.

"It looks like the most effective search engine available now is called 'infinity', and its full address is '*wwl.infinity.mon*', she reported.

"Are you sure, darling? I've never heard of a domain called '*mon*'. What can it stand for, I wonder?"

"Well, if '*com*' stands for 'commercial', then '*mon*' could mean something connected with money perhaps?" Katherine suggested. "Like '*monetary*', say?"

"And how about *wwl*? WWW is obviously "*world wide web*", but '*wwl*'?

"Could still be 'world wide something'... like 'line', or maybe 'loop'?"

"Never mind. We can find out later," said Viktor. "The main question is: can we still do our search for '*multiverse*' or '*multiuniverse*?'

Katherine looked up from her iPad. "I don't see why not. But, on the other hand, there may be no need for it any longer."

"What do you mean, Katia? Why no need?"

"Because... because... I have a feeling that we must have found what we were looking for already."

"How? I don't understand!"

"It looks like we are dealing with a new kind of internet here. And if it is indeed different from what we had until yesterday afternoon, there can be only one explanation – we are on another planet, or even, as your technologically savvy namesake has suggested, in an altogether different universe!"

"Oh, my God… So what does '*wwl*' stand for then?"
"I wish I knew."

From Catherine's Diary

31 June, morning

What a day it was! The craziest in my memory. Worse even than
yesterday when Victor and I had that nasty car accident, and as if that
was not enough, had to cope with the late-evening intrusion by a
couple of our almost exact lookalikes.

Today, however, was even madder, and I decided to start a diary,
so that one day Victor and I will be able to recall all these incredible
events and, with hope, even have a couple of laughs over them.

The day began with a visit by two policemen. I forget their names,
so will refer to them as the Short Cop and the Tall Cop, or simply PC
Tall and PC Short.

They arrived in the morning, probably to make some kind of
announcement, but we never found out what. From the start, the
cops behaved in a rather bizarre way, particularly the tall one who
kept staring at me (and at times at Victor too) so intently with his
grey unblinking eyes that I began to experience serious doubts as to
whether it was indeed myself sitting at the table opposite him.

As soon as we introduced ourselves, the cops suddenly jumped
off their chairs and dashed outside for "a quick word in private", as
PC Tall put it. Victor and I were left to guess what had happened,
whereas yesterday's guests did not even bother to come downstairs
until much later.

Victor and I were hoping that the policemen would never return.
We could then have some peace and attend to our injuries which
were still hurting. But they did barge back in shortly – looking even
more puzzled than before. This is how the conversation went, as far
as I can remember…

"Can you tell us, madam, whose car is parked in your driveway?" PC Short asked me.

"Definitely not ours!" I replied and explained that our old Volvo was badly damaged in yesterday's car accident and was now in a police garage waiting to be repaired.

"So you had a car accident too?" cried out the tall cop with utter disbelief, as if I told him that a UFO had just landed in our backyard.

"What do you mean by 'too'?" It was time for Victor to intervene. "Who else had an accident yesterday?"

"Never mind," mumbled PC Tall and exchanged another puzzled glance with his colleague.

It was at that very moment that Viktor and Katherine came down the stairs. They both looked red-eyed, dishevelled and agitated as if they had just had sex in their bedroom.

"Good morning, officers!" Viktor greeted the policemen. "Please excuse us for not coming down earlier: we needed to check something on the web urgently."

The cops were looking at the Ks with consternation bordering on awe, as if the latter were a couple of apparitions, albeit it was the policemen who both turned ghostly pale, as if they were about to faint.

"You... you were checking something on the web?" PC Short asked after an awkward pause. "Do... do you have spiders in the house or what?"

"I meant we had to do an internet search," explained Viktor.

"So you were checking something on the lace then." said the tall cop who seemed to be able to control his emotions better that his shorter colleague. "What exactly did you look for on the World Wide Lace?"

Viktor suddenly got agitated.

"This is it!" he exclaimed tapping himself on the forehead. "This is what *wwl* stands for – World Wide Lace! You were right, Katia: it looks like we have strayed onto a different planet!"

"Can I ask you to introduce yourselves?" PC Tall asked the Ks.

"Certainly, officer. We are Katherine and Viktor Petroff – married, no children," Viktor replied semi-jokingly. Without realising it, he repeated what Victor, my husband, had said half an hour earlier almost word-for-word.

What happened then, no one could have predicted.

PC Short snatched a gun out of his holster and aimed it at us and the Ks, who were trying to retreat to the corridor. "Freeze, or I will shoot!" he yelled to no one in particular, his eyes gleaming with blind insane rage.

PC Tall pounced on him, and – with a quick practiced kick – knocked the gun out his hand. He then grabbed his colleague by the neck from behind, turned him round, like a large rag doll – and before we could say Jack Robinson – dexterously handcuffed him.

"Sorry, mate," he was muttering. "I won't hurt you. Just to make you safe… for your own good… You've simply lost control for a moment and I don't blame you for that…"

PC Short was trying – unsuccessfully – to liberate himself from his colleague's iron grip. "Reinforcements! We need reinforcements!" he was shouting, his eyes bulging.

PC Tall turned his head towards us. "Look here," he panted out. "I don't know who you are and how come you all look the same, have the same names and are still alive. We'll go now, but we will be back with our CID guys who will sort you all out, I promise. In the meantime, don't you try to escape or hide, for we'll find you anywhere in this universe!"

"How about a parallel one?" Viktor mumbled in a semi-whisper before his wife had time to hush him. Luckily, the policemen appeared not to have overheard him.

PC Tall frog-marched his twitching and foaming colleague out of the cottage and soon – from behind the door left wide ajar by the fleeing policemen – we heard the sound of an engine coming to life.

I looked out of the window just in time to get a glimpse of the police car backing out of our driveway. "**POLISE**" was written in large letters above the vehicle's receding bumper.

For a minute or two, all four of us stayed silent. It was VK who spoke first.

"I think we all should quickly pack up and get out of here before these guys return with more police idiots," he said.

"Nonsense!" my husband Victor exclaimed. "The tall policeman was right: there is nowhere we can hide from them in this universe."

"Let's go back to our own universe, or universes, then!" suggested VK.

"It's easier said than done. Does anyone know how to do that? I certainly don't."

We all remained silent. Then Katherine raised her hand, asking for a permission to speak in a school-like fashion.

"Are we absolutely sure that is what has happened to us? That we have strayed into a different world?"

"Well, how else can you explain the fact that we appear to be the doubles of each other?" VK continued. "And all those little discrepancies in spelling. Then how about the internet, with no google and lots of unfamiliar domains? 'The World Wide Lace', my foot! The world wide mess would be a better name. But the main proof is that I think I now know what happened to our counterparts from the universe where we are now. Remember: the tall cop seemed surprised by what we all looked like and by the fact that we were all still alive which means that the native couple who live or lived in this very cottage and whom we all should have encountered on arrival could have died in a car crash yesterday. That was the reason the cops paid us a visit – to notify of their death. Not one but two of them, as police protocol dictates."

I thought it was time for me to volunteer my humble opinion.

"Viktor is right," I said. "We don't know how to get back. But somebody here may know. There must be scientists in this world too. What we have to do before we can find our native universe is find a university – sorry for the pun – and ask the physicists, cosmologists or mathematicians there if they can help us out. The sooner we do it, the better."

"Don't know about you guys, but I cannot go anywhere this morning," said Katherine. "And the reason is that my mother is supposed to bring Sharik, our poodle, here by midday. She has been looking after him in our absence."

"You mean that YOUR mum is going to bring YOUR dog to OUR house?" I asked and immediately realised how stupid my question must have sounded.

"Enough of that, Cat!" said my husband. "I think we have established already that the cottage is neither ours nor theirs. In a truly Buddhist scenario, it is also both ours and theirs, for in actual fact it belongs to the poor third couple of our lookalikes who must have perished in the car accident yesterday. What's interesting is that my father and Catherine's father- in-law had been looking after OUR WHITE poodle in our absence. I have completely forgotten that he is also due here with the dog by midday. But we cannot wait for him… for them… Catherine is right: we must urgently leave the cottage and head towards the nearest university. That would help us avoid another police invasion too."

"Why don't we phone our respective parents and tell them to come later?" suggested VK taking out his mobile.

"You can use the landline!" Victor, my husband, told him.

"Thank you, sir, for being so kind as to invite me to use my own phone in my own house!" VK bowed in mock reverence.

This time, it was Katherine, his wife, who intervened.

"Come off it, Vitya! You guys are like two fighting cockerels."

"Or rather like one and the same cockerel with a split personality disorder," VK remarked glumly while pressing the keys of his smart phone.

40

From Katherine's Diary:

31 June, afternoon

What a day it was! The craziest in my memory. Worse even than yesterday when Viktor and I had to experience that nasty 'slight' turbulence on our flight from Majorca, and as if that was not enough, on returning home discovered a couple of intruders – our almost exact lookalikes in our cottage.

Today, however, was even madder, and I decided to write a diary, so that one day Viktor and I will be able to recall all these incredible events and, with hope, even have a couple of laughs over them.

The day started with a visit by two policemen, but my husband and I did not have a chance to see them until later, for we were both upstairs – stuck in our puny third bedroom, doubling as an office, doing what was meant to be a simple search on my iPad Mini. We were hoping to find some answers to all those multiple puzzles we had to confront yesterday. What we uncovered during the search, however, was so profoundly mind-boggling that I do not feel capable of writing about it. Not yet. I will simply say that our internet findings did not make any sense whatsoever (at least they didn't to me) and only added to the confusion of the already complicated situation.

From our office-cum-bedroom we could hear our lookalikes talking to the policemen amicably until we heard a man's voice shouting: "So you had a car accident too?" At that point we thought we should come down and see what was going on.

The moment the constables saw Viktor and me, they got very agitated, particularly, the shorter one, who looked and behaved as if he had just escaped from a lunatic asylum. His taller colleague tried to calm him down, but failed and had to – literally – drag him out of the house. Before they both left, the tall policeman ordered all four of us to stay put and promised to return with more of his fellow policemen soon.

When their car was backing out of our driveway, I was able to spot through the window that it had the word '**POLISE**' on its side. Perhaps Viktor's naggings about all those spelling mistakes yesterday were justified to an extent?

After the policemen left, we all had a lively discussion of our common predicament and of what to do next. It was obvious that all four of us (or were there just two of us plus the doubles?) had somehow strayed into the same alternative universe – parallel to our respective ones. It was also obvious that all four (or two) of us were eager to get back to where we came from, but did not know how. It was decided in the end that the moment the policemen left us alone, we would all go to the nearest university to talk to experts in quantum mechanics, cosmology and the probability theory who may be able to tell us how to return back home.

At that point I suddenly remembered that my mum, who had been looking after Sharik, our black poodle, was supposed to bring him back at about midday today. I could not even begin to think what she would make of our doubles sharing the cottage with us and was worried the shock could trigger another heart attack as she had already had two. And, sure enough, Victor, or VC, immediately recalled that his dog, also a poodle, but white, not black, was about to be delivered back home by HIS dad.

In the first case of consensus (for until then the four us could not agree about anything at all), it was decided that both parents – as well as the dogs – must be kept at bay for the time being. We had to urgently tell them NOT to come.

But that proved much harder than we had expected. No matter how many times Viktor, my husband, tried to dial my mum's number, he couldn't get through, and we all had to listen to the "Check the number and try again!" automated message, played from the telephone's speaker, several dozen times until he finally gave up.

And, of course, exactly the same thing happened to VC, when he tried to dial his dad's number.

The time was approaching midday.

"Well, it looks like the parents' visit is now inevitable," VK concluded.

"You never know. It may well happen that only one of them exists in this universe," objected VC.

"Or possibly none at all?" suggested Catherine.

"How about the dogs?" I asked timidly.

"We'll have to wait and see," VC shrugged. "But one thing is clear: to be on the safe side and not to shock too much whatever parent or pet is going to arrive, we must make sure not to appear in front of them together. If it is your mum who comes first, then one of the ladies and a bloke will go upstairs and hide in a bedroom; if it is my dad, well... pretty much the same. He, or she, or they won't be able to tell who is who, for we do look like twin couples. And let's also make sure that we, or you, or whoever, stay there until the parent leaves."

"But what if they arrive simultaneously?" I asked. "What do we do then?"

Victor had no time to respond. We heard the noise of a car entering our driveway. I looked out. Oh, my God: it was followed by another car, literally at its tail! And none of them was a "Police", or a **"Polise"**, for that matter, car either!

The moment they came to a stop, we could hear loud barking from the vehicles. Or maybe from just from one of them – we couldn't tell.

Chapter Six

An Unlikely Reunion

"Oh, my God! I can't believe it! Mama! I thought you had... died!"

Victor, who went to open the door was screaming at the top of his lungs.

Katherine, who was waiting in the lounge as Catherine and VK were running up the stairs to hide in one of the bedrooms, could hear a crackling old woman's voice:

"What is 'died', Vitya?" the woman spoke with a heavy East European accent. "I don't know this English word. If you mean 'ceased', then you are wrong, my boy. It is me, Elvira Petrovas, your Mamma. As you can see and hear, I am very much de-ceased which, as you should know, means 'alive'!"

"And where... where is Papa? He was supposed to bring the dog back..." Victor mumbled.

"Papa? You must be seriously ill, son. Your father ceased nearly twenty years ago. Besides, you never asked me to look after a dog. It's Koshkin, your tabby cat, I had been feeding at my place in your absence."

The woman pointed at a large shopping bag she was holding from where a pair of piercing green eyes stared at Victor with unadulterated feline hatred.

The old woman's tirade was followed first by the characteristic muffled thud of a falling body, then by a fit of loud barking.

Katherine dashed out into the corridor.

Victor was lying supine on the floor, next to the long-suffering 'Welcome' doormat, with his eyes shut. He looked pale but was breathing – he had just fainted with shock. An elderly lady in a black kerchief was kneeling above him and mumbling something incomprehensible, probably in Russian. Behind her stood a tall stooping gentleman in a worn-out tweed jacket, with leather patches on the sleeves. He was squinting at the scene myopically through his old-fashioned pince-nez glasses. His wrinkled right hand was clutching an imitation-leather dog lead, stretched to breaking point by a large spotted Dalmatian – barking for all he was worth.

"Shush, Kirash! Shush!" the man was saying in the doomed manner of someone who understands the futility of his efforts but carries on anyway.

It was now Katherine's turn to get the shock of her life.

"Dad!"

In front of her stood her father Hugo, who had died ten years before. She and Viktor had both attended his funeral at Barnham Crematorium and stayed there until the red curtain was automatically drawn in front of his coffin. No, it could not possibly be him. Who or what then? An illusion? An apparition? A vicious ghost who came to torment her?

Katherine felt dizzy. She suddenly realised that the only way out of this mess was to take the animals and to send the impostor couple away – as fast as possible, before Viktor and Catherine, who were probably still hiding upstairs, got a chance to see them, or – more importantly – before the newcomers themselves, whoever they were, could see the doubles. From the effect such an encounter had on the burly healthy policemen earlier, it was easy to conclude that two frail OAPs – even if consisting purely of ectoplasm, or whatever stuff ghosts are made of – might simply croak there and then.

Later Katherine would find it hard to recall the exact sequence of her thoughts and actions as she – having stepped over her husband's, still horizontal, lookalike – lifted the cat out of the woman's shopping bag and, holding the seemingly unperturbed moggy with her left hand, grabbed Kirash's lead with the other. She then started gently but firmly pushing the visitors out of the cottage, despite their loud protestations, and mumbling something to the effect that an emergency had occurred and they would have to come back for a cup of tea some other time. As she came into close contact with the man claiming to be her deceased dad, she couldn't help sensing that highly peculiar smell, so familiar to her from childhood – the unique dad's smell that had been clinging to her father's clothes as she was sorting them out a couple of months after his death, at which point she came close to giving Hugo, or whoever he was, a big hug. But instead – having mobilised all her emotional strength – she kept pushing him and the old woman out of the cottage and didn't stop until the door closed behind them.

She then returned her attention to Victor and the animals. The dog, having howled and barked at the door for a couple of minutes, tried to chase the cat into the kitchen, but the latter was no easy prey: curving his back into a small fluffy hillock, he retreated under the coat rack and was hissing at his attacker threateningly from behind Katherine's (or Catherine's?) old demi-season jacket.

Ignoring all the barking and hissing, Katherine knelt over Victor – still unconscious. She lifted his head off the floor and held his face with both hands. An experienced medical receptionist, she had undergone extensive first-aid training in case an infirm patient suddenly fainted or felt seriously unwell while waiting for an appointment. First, she made sure Victor was breathing – and he certainly was. She checked for any bleeding – there was none.

Gently, Katherine put Victor's head back on the doormat, and, having grasped his shirt sleeves, turned him to the side – in recovery position. She then moved his left arm and leg outwards to stop him lying flat, bent his elbow and knee, turned his head to the left too and made sure his airways were all clear. To Katherine's slight embarrassment, she couldn't help enjoying touching Victor and thinking of how handsome he was.

"What... what happened?" Victor whispered suddenly, having opened his eyes.

Katherine straightened up resolutely. "Don't worry. You simply blacked out for a minute or so."

"I thought I was asleep and dreamed of my late mum... And what's this noise?" Victor tried to lift his head off the floor.

"They are probably our pets, although the dog that we used to have was a poodle, not a Dalmatian. Your cat is here too."

"We never had a cat," Victor mumbled. "Ours was also a dog – a white poodle called Sharik."

"We too had a poodle called Sharik, but he was black, not white. Wait a moment, what was it that my dead dad was calling him? Kirash? But this IS 'Sharik', only in reverse. God help me... I think I am going to faint too..."

"Did you say – 'my dead dad'?"

"No, I didn't. You must have misheard me." Katherine decided it was best not to shock Victor again.

"And where is the cat from, if none of us used to own one?" he persisted.

"Look, I know as much as you do, so stop asking me questions!" Katherine's patience was running out. "I think it is time to brief our respective... er... partners. They must be still unaware of all the recent developments while sitting quietly upstairs, behind the closed door."

She pointed at the tightly shut door leading to the staircase and to the lounge, and explained: "I closed the door myself so as not to further disturb our recent visitors. I was worried about your wife's and my husband's sanity too."

Katherine helped Victor off the floor. Together they calmed down the animals by locking the dog in the kitchen and letting the cat out of the house "for an afternoon stroll," as Victor put it. "He can make me smile," thought Katherine.

She shouldn't have worried about Catherine and Viktor, who were unaware of all the turbulent events downstairs, for all the while they stayed in an upstairs bedroom. It was there that VC and Katherine found them locked in a passionate embrace.

Chapter Seven

An Unsettling Recollection

"Stop knocking, will you, and do come in!" Superintendent Burgess shouted from behind his desk. Someone had been pounding at the door of his small office.

PC Dawson burst – almost fell – into the room and approached his superior officer unsteadily.

"What's wrong with you, Dawson? Have you been drinking?" the Superintendent demanded.

"I... I... haven't... Sir..." PC Dawson was frantically, yet unsuccessfully, trying to compose himself and was finding it difficult to speak.

"Here, drink this and calm down!" the Superintendent poured some water into an opaque glass on his desk and moved it towards the constable. PC Dawson grabbed the glass with a shaking hand and spilled out half of its contents onto his rumpled uniform, covered with wet white stains, as if someone had vomited on it.

"For God's sake, Dawson, what happened? And where is your colleague PC Hartley?

"He is... he is not feeling well... Had to lock him up in a vacant detention cell for his own safety, Sir..."

"What?" The Superintendent could hardly believe his ears. "You've locked your fellow constable up in a detention cell? And why is your uniform so soiled? What's going on, Dawson?"

It took another five minutes and three more glasses of water for PC Dawson to pull himself together somewhat. Speaking in gasps, as if choking on his own uvula, he recounted the events of that morning.

Prolonged silence ensued. Finally, Superintendent Burgess poured himself a full glass of water and downed it in one gulp.

"Are you sure that the number plates of the car parked in the driveway were the same as those of the vehicle involved in the fatal accident yesterday?" he asked.

"Absolutely sure, Sir! Unlike poor Josh, I am – surprisingly – still sane."

"And you are saying that both couples not only looked very much like each other but were also spitting images of the deceased man and woman in the morgue?"

"I swear on my life, Sir!"

"Hmm…" Superintendent Burgess stood up and was pacing his cubicle of an office nervously.

"If you don't mind me saying this, Sir, I think we must urgently send some CID guys there and have all those people arrested," PC Dawson suggested.

"Arrested for what? For looking like twins? There's no such article in either Criminal or Civilian codes. And what if they ARE indeed just twins – four prankster siblings having a laugh at our expense?"

"Then we should arrest them for wasting police time!"

"Wait a second, Dawson. It was not they who intruded on us. Don't forget that it was you and Hartley who came to see them in their house, not the other way round."

"The house was not theirs, Sir! It belonged to the dead couple!"

"Listen, Sean – I hope you don't mind me calling you Sean – Let's not jump to conclusions. We must certainly investigate this further, but cautiously… by keeping an eye on those four without arousing their suspicions."

"What if they escape? What then?"

"Yes, we must find a way of keeping them inside the cottage for as long as possible. Imagine the kind of furore they can stir up if all four of them appear in a public place, like, say, a local branch of Tesda supermarket, together? The media will be after them in a jiffy! I think I've got an idea of how we can persuade them to stay put.

Don't worry, Sean – I am taking this matter under my personal control. Your shift is nearly over, so why don't you go home, take a long hot bath and have some sleep? But before you do that, please check on PC Hartley in that detention cell and see if he needs medical attention."

"Thank you, Sir!" nodded PC Dawson and reached for the door handle, but the Superintendent stopped him.

"Before you go, Dawson, tell me again what was the exact response of one of the men in the cottage when you said you'd hunt them down anywhere in this universe?"

"He mumbled something like 'how about a parallel one?' A rather cheeky thing to say to a police officer on duty, if you ask me, Sir. The man probably thought I didn't hear him, but I did, I did!"

Superintendent Burgess stood near the window in his tiny office staring at a patch of littered suburban forest behind it. He was trying to recall the events of twenty-five odd years earlier when he, a recent graduate of the Police School, was a trainee constable at Woodhill Police Station in North London. One summer evening, they received a call from a receptionist of the local Travel Inn Hotel who claimed to be having problems with registering a foreign guest and was in need of assistance. The lady sounded distressed, so the duty sergeant assigned PC Burgess to go and sort it out.

When he arrived at the scene, he was greeted by a middle-aged receptionist, whose name was either Sheila or Sharon, Burgess could not remember exactly. Her eyes were red and tearful, as if she had been crying. Across the counter from her stood an exasperated gentleman in a an expensive-looking well-tailored suit. He was tall and slender, with a distinguished mane of snow-white hair and piercing deep-blue eyes. As is often the case with albinos, his age was pretty hard to establish from just looking at him, but young PC Burgess thought then that the man was unlikely to be much younger than forty or much older than fifty-five.

"Good evening. I am PC Burgess. Please tell me what happened," he said to the pair.

The receptionist spoke first.

"This gentleman came in about an hour ago and asked if we had a room for him. He didn't have a reservation, but we are normally not too busy this time of the year, and there was one junior suite that was vacant, so I offered it to him. As the guest was obviously a foreigner, the fact that I grasped from his accent, I asked him to fill in the form with his passport details, as required by law, which he did. But when I looked at the completed form, it made no sense whatsoever."

"What do you mean it made no sense?" PC Burgess asked.

"See for yourself, officer!" said the receptionist. From her desk, she picked up a sheet of paper, covered with uneven ant-like scribbles – small but perfectly legible – and handed it over to the policeman who read the form with growing disbelief.

Twenty-five odd years later, even Superintendent Burgess, with his legendary photographic memory, would not have been able to visualise that amazing document clearly, with all the numbers and dates, which suddenly seemed very important to him.

After some frantic rubbing of his forehead, Burgess returned to his desk, bent down and pulled the shiny brass handle of the bottom desk drawer, where he covertly kept photocopies of the most peculiar and memorable documents of his policing career, and tried to pull it out.

"Damn it!" The drawer, which was last opened several years earlier, was locked: it was, strictly speaking, against the rules to keep official documents, or their copies, anywhere but the station archives, but Burgess, who had been hoping to write a book about his policing career one day, stored them there at his own risk. His only hope was that the mysterious foreigner's registration form would be among them as one of the most bizarre documents he had ever come across.

Having ferreted out a bunch of old keys from a small safe in the corner, Burgess tried each of them methodically but none seemed to fit. When there was just one rusty little key left untried, the policeman began to despair, yet it was that very last key that fit the keyhole, and turned in it slowly, as if unwillingly.

"Eureka!" Burgess pulled out the drawer and rummaged through the dusty brown folders. The faded yellowish photocopy of the sought-after hotel registration form was of course at the very bottom of the pile, straight underneath a written statement he once took from a drunk driver that consisted of just three words: "I am plastered!"

Having snatched the form out of the drawer, Superintendent Burgess switched on his green desktop lamp and began to read:

<u>Travel Inn Hotel Guest Registration Form</u>

First Name: Navi

Last Name: Vonavi

Day/Month/Year of Birth: 61st of Lipra, 3491

Place of Birth: The village of Kadus, Tavrida

Nationality: Tavridian

Place of Residence: Vokrakh, Tavrida

Place of Work: National Bank of Tavrida

Position: Head of Operations

Car Number Plate: n/a

Date of Arrival in the UK: 91st of Rebmevon, 9891

Intended Date of Departure: 42nd of Rebmevon, 9891

Signature..

"Hmm…" Burgess put aside the form, closed his eyes, as if with exhaustion (and he suddenly felt very tired indeed) and re-immersed himself into his reveries…

"Can I see your passport, sir?" PC Burgess asked the stranger then.

"Please yourself!" the man barked out and all but threw the document in a battered green leather wallet at the policeman. He spoke with a soft foreign accent which sounded similar to French.

Burgess took the passport out of the wallet. Three long words in an unfamiliar script resembling Cyrillic were printed in faded gold letters across the cover. Underneath – in smaller letters – was the English translation: **'People's Republic of Tavrida'**. Unlike the registration form, with all its dates and numbers, Burgess was able to visualise the man's passport very clearly, as if it was lying in front of him on the desk.

On the first page, resplendent with watermarks, was the stranger's head shot, half-concealed under a large round stamp, with more foreign letters in it. More 'Cyrillic' was underneath the photo and on each of the subsequent pages of the passport.

It was all Greek to Burgess until on pages three and four he spotted a cluster of UK arrival and departure stamps – all properly signed and dated.

"So, you've been to the UK before?" he asked the foreigner.

"Of course I have! Dozens of times! Britain is my country's leading commercial partner and as a banker I do everything I can to facilitate our co-operation."

"And did you travel with the same passport then, Sir?" asked young PC Burgess and immediately realised how superfluous his question was: he had just seen the stamps himself.

"Of course, I have! Many times. And never before has there been a problem!"

"This is very strange, Sir. To begin with, as far as I know, Tavrida, the country you claim to be from, simply does not exist."

"What do you mean it doesn't exist?" the stranger exploded. "Yes, our population is relatively small, just over five million, but my country has a rich history stretching over a thousand years, and a very well-developed modern infrastructure."

"You don't happen to have a map of the world?" PC Burgess asked the receptionist.

"I have a small one in my diary," she replied.

"Can I see it? Thanks."

He unfolded the map on the reception desk and invited the stranger to pinpoint Tavrida on it.

The foreigner looked increasingly puzzled when, after five minutes of scrutinising the map, he failed to locate his native country.

"It must be some kind of mistake," he was muttering, with drops of sweat glistening on his forehead. "On all the maps I have seen before, Tavrida was just about here!"

He was pointing at the Crimean Peninsula which then was still part of Russia and wasn't annexed by Georgia.

Burgess was at a loss and needed to consult his superiors, but it was getting late and he didn't feel like bothering his bosses at that hour with something that was most probably just a sophisticated journalistic prank, aimed at the hotel – or maybe even at the police – by one of the tabloid newspapers. If that was the case, imagine how stupid he would look. Not a good way to start a police career.

The best thing was to wait until morning, so Burgess persuaded the receptionist to put the mysterious visitor up in one of the vacant rooms, number 33, just for one night. When the door closed behind the foreigner, the young policeman installed himself in an armchair in the hotel corridor from where he could see the door of room 33 very clearly, and braced himself for a sleepless night.

He did succeed in staying awake until the morning and could vouch that no-one had left or entered the stranger's room. But when at 8 am he and the receptionist knocked at its door, there was no reply. After ten minutes of futile pounding, Burgess broke the lock and burst in. The room was empty and the substantial double bed in the middle appeared untouched. Not a trace of the foreigner or his belongings could be found. The visitor from Tavrida simply vanished.

After the initial shock, PC Burgess and the receptionist agreed to stay mum about the incident which, as they both decided, was probably but a short-lived collective hallucination. To be on the safe side, Burgess took a short statement from the distraught woman. Back at the station, he jotted down his own one-page report about the incident and filed it together with receptionist's statement in an empty folder, which had a number but no name. He then buried the thin folder in the bottom drawer of his desk, under piles of others – mostly driving-offence-related folders and case reports. When his commanding officer enquired casually about the incident at the hotel, Burgess shrugged and mumbled something about a nuisance call from a drunken guest which he decided not to pursue, for by the time he arrived at the hotel, the latter had already checked out and left.

But the policeman did not give up on the case completely. From school, he was friendly with Daniel Spiegeltent, a somewhat nerdy lad, who had always been brilliant in maths and went to become Professor of Mathematics at Camford University by the age of twenty-seven. If anyone could throw any light onto the mysterious stranger, it was him.

Burgess rang his school friend and arranged to meet in a small quiet pub opposite his police station.

Spiegeltent listened to PC Burgess' story without interrupting and then spent a very long time studying a copy of the Tavridian's registration form, that very copy that was now – over a quarter of a century later – staring at Burgess from his desk. Looking at it, the Superintendent was now able to recall his conversation with Spiegeltent in every minute detail.

The policeman was finishing his second pint of draft Hannes, a kind of black Scottish porter, when Daniel finally looked up from the form.

"This is incredible!" he muttered, visibly shocked by what he had just seen.

"What… what is inc-inc-redible?" asked PC Burgess nearly choking on the last sip of Hannes.

"All of it, but first and foremost – all those 'Lipras' and 'Rebmevons'."

"What's so incredible ab-ab-out them?" the policeman was now suffering from a hiccupping fit. "They are just the names of the m-months in his alleged country… T-tavrida…"

"I have grasped that much," Spiegeltent said quietly. "But have you tried to read these words from right to left?"

"What for? OK, let me see… Lip-pra… Lip-pra… It reads 'Ap… ril'. April! And 'Rebmevon'… Nov… n-nov… em… ber… November! What the hell?"

"Indeed. But this is not all," his friend continued. "If you read the years of his birth and the date of his arrival here from right to left – what do we end up with?"

"'61st of Lipra, 3491.' Wait a moment… It becomes the '16th of April 1943' – meaning that the guy was… is… just over forty-five years old. That makes perfect sense – he looked it!" PC Burgess exclaimed.

"And do take notice of his arrival and intended departure dates," the scientist continued. "What year is it now?"

"1989," said the policeman.

"What month?"

"N-november!" PC Burgess was stuttering again, this time not from the Hannes but from extreme puzzlement.

"Precisely! If read in reverse order, the dates would indicate that the stranger had arrived in our country on the 19th of November 1989 and was intending to leave on the 24th! What date is it today?"

"The 20th of N-november," blurted out the policeman.

"Here we go! The foreigner arrived in the UK six days ago, with the intention to stay for ten days which he probably would have done, had you not frightened him off with your assertions that the country he had come from doesn't exist!"

"But, Daniel, it doesn't! It doesn't!" shouted PC Burgess.

"Calm down, mate," Spiegeltent said soothingly. "It may not exist in our world, but in his it probably does."

"What do you mean? Don't we all live in one and the same bloody old world?"

Instead of replying, Spiegeltent stood up and put on his coat.

"I have to go now," he said. "The question you've just asked cannot be answered in just a few words. So why don't you pop in to my office at the uni sometime tomorrow afternoon? We could carry on talking then – and I will also show you a couple of things you may find of interest."

Well, it so happened that the following day a particularly nasty crime – a jealousy-related double murder – was committed in Muswell End, and PC Burgess was assigned to investigate it as his first murder investigation ever, so he never had a chance to visit his scholarly friend's office. The daily routine of the busy police station soon took over his life. Slowly but surely Burgess kept climbing up the service ladder all the way to being appointed Superintendent at a large police station in Camford, the same town where – coincidentally – his friend Spiegeltent's university tenure was taking place. With time, the story of the mysterious visitor from Tavrida had receded farther and farther back in his mental priorities list – up to the point when it was almost entirely forgotten. It was only now that he had had a flashback.

He needed to get in touch with Daniel Spiegeltent, Superintendent Burgess decided. But prior to that, he would pay a visit to the twin couples' household himself.

Burgess replaced the registration form in the folder carefully, and pushed the drawer shut without locking it. He then dialled the duty officer and asked if there was a spare car in the station's garage. "I will only need it for an hour or so," he said.

Chapter Eight

Slaps and Snogs

"What's going on here?" Victor shouted at the snoggers.

Catherine and Viktor stopped kissing and let go of each other. Catherine stood up from a small bedroom couch on which they had both been sitting, or rather reclining, and straightened up her clothes. She was breathing heavily. With her face flushed, her long brown hair tussled and her large green eyes veiled up with a touch of gentle dawn-like red, she looked beautiful, as Victor, her husband, had to conclude. That only increased his fury.

"You dirty whore!" he yelled at his wife. "While this nice woman..." he pointed at Katherine who stood behind him in the doorway and looked no less shocked than himself, "...while this woman and I were fighting off our common ghosts down there, in the corridor, you found nothing better to do than snog a complete stranger!"

"I... I... don't know what happened to me..." whispered Catherine. "I thought... I thought for a moment that it was you, darling..." she pointed at VK who was still sitting on the couch with his head down.

"Cut the crap!" VC snapped. "You bloody hell knew it was NOT me, you slut!"

"Watch your tongue, you brute, when talking to a lady!" VK muttered from the couch. He kept staring at the floor and did not bother to look up at VC, as if the latter did not exist.

"How dare you? She is MY wife, after all!" he screamed.

"Yes, but if we stick with your own parallel worlds theory, whereby we are not different individuals but just doubles, the versions of one and the same person, she is MY wife too. Just like that lady behind you, is YOUR wife as well as mine!"

It was now Katherine's turn to speak.

"Stop clowning, Vitya!" she said to her husband sternly. "You start sounding like some nasty oriental sultan in a harem in dispute with another polygamist sultan over some submissive little concubines. It is truly disgusting, guys, for Catherine and I also have feelings. Why can't you just face up to it and say, yes, I was about to commit adultery with a woman who looked very much like my wife."

VK finally looked up.

"But that's precisely my point, Katya. Kissing your exact double does not constitute adultery. It is almost like… like kissing YOU, I suppose…"

"I've had enough! If that brute on the couch refuses to stop yap-yapping, I am going to shut him up by force!" announced VC to no one in particular. He then briskly paced across the room and – with the open palm of his right hand – slapped VK in the face.

What followed was totally against everyone's expectations. Despite a loud and seemingly powerful slap, VK continued to sit on the couch with his head down, as if oblivious of the commotion around him, whereas VC who had delivered the blow, was howling in pain. A bright and quickly spreading purple spot appeared on his left cheek.

"What the hell! It feels as if I had hurt myself accidentally!" he mumbled, ready to wail with pain.

It was Katherine who came up to him and took his head in her hands.

"Quite a blow it was… Wait a second, Vitya," she said.

She ran downstairs to the kitchen, soaked her hanky under the cold water tap and, having returned to the bedroom, pressed it against VC's burning cheek.

"Thank you, Katia!" smiled Victor. "You are so warm and caring that I feel like giving you a big hug. May I?"

And without waiting for permission, he pressed Katherine to his chest and kissed her on the forehead.

That was too much for VK to take. Having jumped up from the couch, he approached VC from the back and grabbed him by the throat.

Again – the result was totally unexpected. While VC was continuing to squeeze Katherine, as if nothing happened, VK himself collapsed on the floor and was gasping for breath.

"Can we all just stop hurting each other? Is there anyone sane here?" Catherine, who had hardly uttered a word until then, shouted suddenly.

So piercing and desperate was her scream that her three companions were unable to ignore it. Her husband and Katherine unlocked their embrace and looked at her silently. VK got up from the floor rubbing his neck and was staring at her too.

"Can't you see what's going on?" Catherine continued. "We can cuddle and kiss each other, but as soon as we try to hurt one another, we end up hurting ourselves!"

"I am not sure I understand what you mean," mumbled VK.

"I am disappointed in you, Vitya. Well, if you need another proof, come up here and try to hit my husband again."

"Hit your husband again? But we are now sort of square, so to speak. Why would I want to do it again?"

"Well, if you like me, do as I say. Come closer and hit him, just like he hit you two minutes ago – I beg you!"

"Well… if you insist…"

VK paced up to VC, who now – for some reason – stood at attention in front of him, and timidly touched his face.

"No, this is not good enough. Hit him harder!" Catherine insisted.

VK clumsily – and still fairly gently – punched VC in the solar plexus – and immediately bent down in pain while VC stood above him unhurt.

"Well, do you see it now, or do you want another try?" she asked him sarcastically.

"No, I can… can see it," VK had to gasp for breath again. "I can see it, but I still don't understand what it means."

"Well, in this case, I hope my dear husband will be able to explain it to you. He knows more about parallel worlds than I do. Over to you, Vitya!"

"Well, the fact that whenever we try to physically hurt one another, we actually hurt ourselves is the strongest proof so far that my theory is correct," said VC. "The problem is that whereas it appears to ourselves and – judging by the policemen's behaviour – to others too that there are four of us in this cottage, in reality there are just two!"

"What do you mean 'just two'?" interrupted VK, who had only just begun to regain his breath. "Which two are the real us and which aren't?"

"According to quantum theory, one and the same particle, or a cluster of particles, can simultaneously exist in two or more different dimensions or universes, so all four of us can be both real and unreal – all at the same time," said VC. "Yet in truth and despite all those insignificant differences and discrepancies, we are neither twins nor doubles, but just one and the same couple who had bumped into themselves from a different world. And whereas God – or Einstein – whoever created this improbable situation is happy for us to do nice things to one another – like, indeed, kissing or cuddling – the strong self-preservation law, or call it instinct, does not allow us – as quantum creatures – to hurt our opposite numbers, that is ourselves, for in theory physical destruction of one would inevitably mean annihilation of his or her parallel-universe counterpart."

"In short, make love, not war!" VK commented grimly.

"Precisely! We simply don't have a choice," VC shrugged.

"Mmm… I'd rather fancy a kind of *menage a quatre*," said VK.

"In your dreams!" That was Katherine rebuffing her playful husband. "You men always secretly dream of orgies, but women – and I am sure Catherine here will agree with me – are much more moral."

"Your high morals didn't stop you from snogging that chappie for all you were worth!" VK commented.

"I don't know what came over me… As I said, I kind of thought it was YOU. And it was just some innocent kissing, not the wild orgy you are dreaming about."

"But it WAS him! As well as me!" said VC. "You have nothing to feel guilty about. Just like you" – he turned to VK – "for hugging my wife."

"You know what: I don't like it one bit!" Catherine intervened. "We've known each other for less than one day – and look at the mess we are all in already. This whole thing is going to end up very badly unless we find a way of returning to our respective worlds – and fast!"

"Easier said than done," chuckled Victor. "But I do agree: we must get out of here somehow."

"To begin with, let's get out of this cottage before the policemen come back with reinforcements," said VK.

"Why should I run away from MY home?" asked Katherine. "And where to?"

"Well, it is also MY home, and I do agree with your husband: we must find someone who could tell us how to get back to where we came from."

"We have decided to try the nearest uni, haven't we?" said Victor. "Come on then, let's roll before they stop us."

That very moment, a loud rattling noise could be heard from the downstairs kitchen. It was followed by the sound of breaking glass and some frantic barking.

"Oh, my God!" exclaimed Katherine. "We forgot about the pets!"

"Which pets? I didn't think we had any in my house at the moment. And we only have one pet anyway – a dog called Sharik, but he was in the care of my mum while we were in Majorca," said Catherine.

"You were so busy snogging that fellow that you didn't even get a glimpse of the two OAPs who just paid us a visit," VC, her husband, noted sarcastically.

"And it was actually not your mum, but an old man who dropped the dog called Kirash on our doorstep. He was accompanied by an elderly lady with a cat, so we had to accept the moggy too and locked them both up in the kitchen," Katherine explained.

"Who did you lock up – the OAPs?" inquired VK.

"Not funny, Vitya!" his wife said dryly. "The old man and the lady were in a hurry, so I let them go, but the pets had to stay."

"Well, there's no time to worry about the pets," VC concluded. "We must leave the cottage this very moment. I will let the dog out for a run in the garden. As for the cat, let him walk by himself, or herself. Come on, let's hurry up. The car – whoever it belongs to – is still in the driveway. I will drive!"

"Can I sit in the back, next to your wife?" VK asked with a nasty grin.

Chapter Nine

A Geographical Flashback

It took Superintendent Burgess less than half an hour to reach the cottage. To his dismay, there was no car in the driveway, and the house itself appeared empty.

"Could it be that the constables just got drunk and invented the whole story?" he thought momentarily.

Having pressed the doorbell five or six times, Burgess was about to get back into his car and drive away. It was his policeman's instinct – the hard-to-explain 'sixth sense' of an old sleuth – that stopped him.

"I'll sort it out with a magistrate later," he decided, taking a special policeman's skeleton key out of his pocket.

The lock opened at the first try. Having looked stealthily right and left, Burgess let himself inside the cottage and clicked the door shut.

It was one of the standard mass-produced dwellings, built by the government in an attempt to cope with the severe housing crisis the country experienced in the aftermath of World War Four. The interior features and the layout were familiar to Burgess, who himself grew up in a similar cottage in Kentshire. Realising only too well that he may not have a lot of time at his disposal, the policeman took out a torch (it was getting dark outside) and started searching for clues. Clues to what? He wasn't quite sure.

The corridor looked messy, as if there had been a scuffle – with coats, boots and shoe brushes scattered all over it. A rumpled old rug near the door was dirty – with dog's or cat's footprints on it. Burgess peeped into the kitchen but had to withdraw involuntarily at the sight of a huge green-eyed tabby cat sitting in state on top of a kitchen desk, like a monument to itself, and hissing threateningly.

The lounge was in a somewhat better state. Half-finished cups of tea were on the table. Burgess noted with a hint of satisfaction that there were four of them – a fact that gave some credibility to PC Dawson's story.

Stained mugs with soaked tea bags offered no clues to whatever Burgess was hoping to uncover, and he decided to try his luck upstairs, in the bedrooms.

Having quickly inspected all three of them, he found nothing of immediate interest in the smallest one which was probably used as an office. A battered laptop on a small desk near the window could provide some information, but Burgess had neither time nor desire to hack into it. Not now.

In each of the remaining two bedrooms, where – judging by the rumpled sheets and deflated pillows on top of unmade beds – the cottage dwellers must have spent the night, he spotted two almost identical grey suitcases – both unlocked, yet not fully unpacked.

"This could be something!" thought the policeman. Having zipped up the trunks hastily, he dragged them downstairs into the lounge – the best-lit room in the cottage – and started rummaging through their contents, throwing aside small piles of nearly identical lingerie and fluffy balls of unclean socks.

His attention was briefly drawn to the men's shirts, some of which – in both suitcases – were of familiar brands, yet with peculiar spelling mistakes on the labels: 'Kalvin Klein', instead of 'Calvin Clein', 'Lacoste', instead of 'Lakoste' and 'Hugo Boss', with a double 's' at the end instead of one.

The same was true of the mascara samples – 'Chanel', instead of 'Shanel', 'Lancome', instead of 'Lencom'.

At the bottom of each bag there was a guide book. Burgess picked up one, published by 'Rough Planet'. 'A Guide Book to Majorka' was printed on the glossy flap. The second book from the other suitcase was published by 'Daebeker Verlag' and had the title 'A Guidebook to Mayorca'.

"How extraordinary!" Burgess said aloud, his voice echoing in the low-beamed ceiling of the lounge room.

Yet the most amazing find was waiting for him in a side pocket of one of the suitcases. Having unzipped it, he ferreted out a small dog-eared paperback – 'A Concise Atlas of the World'.

"At least, there are no typos on the title page," thought the policeman, opening the Atlas at a random spread. "Eastern and Central Europe" read Burgess, secretly rejoicing at the fact that – again – it was all spelled correctly. "Could it be that I simply imagined the typos in the guidebooks? Or maybe the suitcase owners are some kind of weird collectors of books with boo-boos?" He remembered visiting a museum of newspaper flops in Antwerdam a couple of years earlier.

The Superintendent's relief was short-lived, for there – stuck between Ukraine and Turkey – was a purple stretch of an oblong and largely unfamiliar country. "The People's Republic of Tavrida" was printed all across the designated space.

He opened the title page to check the year of publication, and there it was: 8891!

Superintendent Burgess felt dizzy and dropped the book onto the floor.

"The City of Camford Twinned with Munberg, Germany," read the road sign.

"Not far now," said Victor from behind the wheel.

"For all I know, these university towns can be hugely spread out," remarked Katherine from the passenger seat next to the driver.

"They certainly can be," her husband agreed from the back. "Camford is still not as bad as Oxridge. I get lost there each time I visit it on an assignment."

"Just keep driving, Vitya," Catherine said soothingly to her husband from the seat directly behind him. "And will you kindly remove your hand from my thigh, mister!"

The latest remark – in a voice that was not at all soothing, but irritated and high-pitched – was aimed not at VC, but at VK sitting next to her.

"How dare you, Vitya?" Katherine turned back to look at her husband. "Can't you at least save your lust until later, when – hopefully – we'll know where we are and what to do next?"

"And who we are too," VK echoed. "I am sorry, Katia, I did it mechanically, for it seemed to me for a moment that it was you sitting next to me: same figure, same skirt, same face…"

"Stop this nonsense!" shouted Victor while involuntarily pressing down the accelerator pedal. "It is my wife's legs, not face, that you've been groping! I am going to pull over now and punch you in the face!"

"And you will end up hitting yourself, remember?" his wife intervened. "So why don't you just hit yourself in the face and keep driving? And don't worry. I can stand up for myself just fine!"

"Are you trying to protect him? I can't believe it!" Victor was so exasperated he momentarily let go of the wheel. The car veered to the right and the front wheel hit the curb. All four jumped in their seats. Victor pressed the brake and tried to reverse, but it was too late: the wheel rotated with a characteristic flip-flop sound of a punctured tyre. He pulled over and switched off the engine.

"Happy now?" he asked no one in particular while staring straight in front of himself.

"Not a big deal. Just a flat tyre," VK commented from the back.

"Yes, compared to the real cottage owners we are very lucky," Catherine agreed.

"You mean we are not dead?" said Katherine. "You know what: I am not so sure. At times, I am so confused that I feel I'd rather be dead than face this endless mess. And now – another bloody car accident, just when we are in a hurry to find the university before the police find us!"

VK patted VC on the shoulder: "Hey, can you fix the tyre? It was all your fault, after all."

"I probably can, but I've never had a chance to try," replied Victor. "As to whose fault it was, I think the culprit is obvious. I didn't try to feel your wife's legs, did I?"

"Stop it, guys. Here you go again – like two fighting roosters. Or just one rooster in two incarnations." The voice of reason was coming from Catherine. "It will take you ages to replace the tyre, this is obvious, and we probably cannot even call the AA, for up to now all our attempts at phoning have come to nothing. This place doesn't seem to have normal telephone connections."

"What is AA?" asked VK. "You probably mean AR which stands for automobile recovery?"

"Doesn't matter. I suggest we abandon the car and walk to the uni – it can't be that far away," Catherine continued. "We could then try to fix the problem on the way back."

"Ay-ay, ma'am!" VK raised his hand in a mock army salute. "Let's move out and then move on!"

"And then move in, only I wish I knew where to!" VC concluded, to his wife's barely concealed annoyance.

All four of them climbed out of the Volvo and, having stretched their arms and legs, set off along the quiet suburban street towards the city centre.

Chapter Ten

A Statement and a Scuffle

Having picked the Atlas up from the floor, Superintendent Burgess put it in his pocket. He then tossed the bundles of rumpled clothes and dirty underwear back into the suitcases, not bothering too much with what belonged where, zipped the trunks up hastily and carried them upstairs. He was doing it all mechanically, as if in a kind of a trance, all the while trying to recall the details of his encounter with the mysterious Man from Tavrida twenty-five years ago. And just like earlier that afternoon in his office, Burgess had to acknowledge, with growing anxiety, that he was no longer able to bring back certain small, yet suddenly very important, details, like where exactly the visitor had crossed the UK border and which other places he could have visited before turning up at that particular hotel. His own report about the incident, which he never submitted to his commanding officer, could offer some answers, provided of course the document had been properly filed and still kept in the Woodhill Police Station's archives. The filing system they used in the pre-World Wide Lace years was not brilliant, to say the least, with numerous case files lost as a result.

And although not particularly superstitious, Burgess kept – almost involuntarily – crossing and uncrossing his fingers on top of the steering wheel as he was driving through the sunset burning above the country lanes to his old police station in the outskirts of London, about thirty-five miles away from Camford.

As it turned out, he was in luck. The thin file, consisting of just two documents, was still there – inside an anonymous, yet numbered, light-brown folder stuck between two domestic violence reports –

there was no shortage of such incidents in his former North London precinct. As opposed to posh South London, North London suburbs like Hamgate, Highstead and Muswell End were notoriously rough and poverty-ridden.

Burgess signed the folder out at the station archivist's desk and drove back to Camford. Back at his station, he carried the documents upstairs to his office where he could study them quietly, without interruptions.

Sipping a cup of pale and suspiciously foamy coffee from an old drinks dispensing machine in the station's corridor, he scrutinised the faded pages under the light of a bright table lamp with a green lampshade.

He skipped through his own report and took out the statement of the hapless hotel receptionist which he himself asked her to write after the guest's inexplicable disappearance from his room:

STATEMENT
Taken by PC Peter Burgess of Woodhill Police Station on the 20th of November 1989 from Sheila Purley, receptionist at Travel Inn Hotel

I started my evening shift at the reception desk in the lobby at 6 pm. It was the middle of the week, and we were not very busy. The hotel was half-full and I was not expecting any more guests. At about 7.15 a gentleman arrived. Dressed in an expensive-looking well-tailored suit, he was tall and slender, with a distinguished mane of snow-white hair and piercing deep-blue eyes. As it is often the case with albinos, his age was pretty hard to establish by just looking at him, but I thought that he was unlikely to be much younger than forty or much older than fifty-five.

The man appeared tired and somewhat confused – looking around worriedly, like a troubled bird... ("The receptionist must have been nurturing some literary ambitions," Superintendent Burgess thought on reaching that part of the statement).

I asked the man if he had a reservation, and he said no, sorry, but could he please have a room, for he was very tired after a full day of travels. He spoke with a soft foreign accent – French or possibly German. I replied that he was lucky, for we did have a vacant room for him. In fact, we had half a dozen unoccupied rooms, but our rules dictate that we never say to the guests that the hotel is half-empty, for this may put them off staying with us in future.

The gentleman appeared relieved to hear the news. "This is great!" he said and added: "Can't wait to take a shower and have a nice long sleep."

I gave him the registration form to fill in and asked – just to keep the conversation going: "And where are you travelling from today, Sir?" (Burgess took a big sip of coffee and turned over the page impatiently).

"Well, I would normally fly straight to the UK from my country," he said, "but this time I made a little detour to Majorca before coming here: just desperately needed a long weekend on the beach after a very busy month at the office... To start feeling human again."

"Oh, I like Majorca," I replied, again just out of politeness, "particularly this time of the year when it is past peak season and not too crowded, but the sea is still warm. Where did you stay there?"

"Not far from Palma," the gentleman said, without looking up from the form he was still filling in. "In a very nice hotel with its own small beach."

I didn't question him any further on that matter."

"So, it was Majorca!" Superintendent Burgess shouted triumphantly to no one in particular. He closed the folder and took it to the station's antediluvian Xorex copying machine in the corridor trying to make sense of what he had just learned.

From the typo-prone guide-books and the Atlas found in one of the couple's suitcases, it was clear that they had all been holidaying in Majorca, or Mayorka – whatever the spelling. It was now obvious that twenty-five or so years earlier, the Man from Tavrida visited Majorca too. He could have left his 'Concise Atlas of the World' in a hotel room, where it could have been found by a chambermaid and added to the hotel's book exchange library. One of the couples must have spotted it there twenty-five years later and – either by mistake or deliberately, for one was allowed and even encouraged to take any library item home having replaced it with another book – put it in their suitcase. But why Majorca? Was it a rather bizarre coincidence, or was there another – more solid – reason behind this synchronicity?

"It's a pity the receptionist did not ask the man which hotel he was staying at while in Majorca," Burgess was thinking as the old Xorex was slowly, as if reluctantly, spitting out the copied documents. "The only thing we know is that it had its own small beach. There must be dozens of hotels with their own beaches around Palma, and all of them are bound to have exchange libraries."

Having finished copying, he popped into the post room and asked a courier on duty to take the original folder back to the Woodhill station's archives. He then headed back to his office. As he was unlocking the door with one hand while holding onto the copied documents with another, he suddenly realised that there was still a chance of finding out the name of the hotel where the Man from Tavrida had left his Atlas – by interviewing one of the twin couples, who must have picked it up. At that point in time, he wouldn't have been able to explain what exactly he was hoping to find at that hotel, but his policeman's instinct was telling him that it was important for solving the mystery of both the lookalike couples and the Man from Tavrida.

Burgess was about to leave the office and head home when the phone on his desk ran peremptorily. It was the duty constable from the downstairs reception.

"We have two couples here, just detained and brought in by a patrol car from the Camford Arms where they, allegedly, started a brawl. Shall I call PC Dawson or another officer to question them?"

"Don't bother Dawson. He's just back from a difficult raid and needs rest. I am going to talk to the detainees myself shortly, but in the meantime please ask Sergeant Draper to take them to the interview room and get their names, addresses and all that usual stuff," said Burgess.

He was ready to put the phone down.

"Before you go, just one more thing, boss," the duty constable continued. "These two couples are twins."

"Four twins? Do you mean quadruplets? Do they all look the same – all four?" Burgess asked.

"No. There are two males looking like each other, and two near-identical females. Both couples claim they are married."

"I am on my way!" the Superintendent said with sudden cheerfulness.

He was definitely in luck today, he thought. One of those rare cases when the mountain did come to Muhammad first!

"Are you still there?" he asked the duty constable before hanging up. An idea suddenly occurred to him. "Could you please make sure that fingerprints are taken from all four of them? Yes, as a matter of urgency please! I'd like to see them ASAP!"

Having said that, he put the phone down and ran out of the room.

Let us now travel five or six hours back in time and catch up with the two couples as they walked purposefully along a straight suburban street in Camford after a minor road accident that forced them to abandon their car.

The tree-lined boulevard appeared deserted, despite the constant flow of traffic in its middle. Victor and Katherine led the way, with Viktor and Catherine following at some distance.

The road seemed endless, with no houses or any other landmarks, apart from a lonely pub sign sticking out from behind the trees a hundred or so metres ahead.

"Gosh, it's hot as hell and I am dying for a pint," said Victor. He stopped and mopped his forehead with a handkerchief.

"We must keep walking. The sooner we get to the university, the better," replied Katherine without looking at him.

"Why such a rush? It is lunch time anyway and there won't be anyone there," Victor kept whingeing.

"You are just like my husband – stubborn as a spoilt child!" commented Katherine.

The other couple caught up with them.

"What's happening? Why did you stop?" asked Catherine.

"Your husband says he can't carry on without a pint," Katherine sighed.

"On this particular point, I am happy to agree with my… er… opposite number," intervened Viktor.

"Men… you are all the same," Katherine muttered.

"Not quite the same, but very similar!" smiled Victor. "The first round is on me!"

It was cool and dark inside the Camford Arms – a welcome relief after the blazing heat of the early summer afternoon. The pub was nearly empty. At a small table in the corner, an elderly couple were finishing their discounted late lunch of fish, chips and apple crumble. Half a dozen or so ruddy-faced lunch-time drinkers sat at the bar. They all turned towards the newcomers.

Followed by the patrons' stares, Catherine made her way towards the till.

"Are you still doing food?" she asked the barmaid – a buxom middle-aged woman in a rumpled once-white apron.

"Too late for that, love!" the barmaid replied. "Can only offer you crisps and cracklings."

"Who cares about food? I am quite happy to have a liquid lunch!" proclaimed Victor from behind his wife's back.

"And I wouldn't mind having some crisps with my pint," stated Viktor, as he caught up with the Cs at the counter.

"As for me, I'd rather go for the cracklings. They are full of protein and actually, despite what many people think, are quite good for your health – I am telling you this as a medical receptionist!" announced Katherine.

This conversation was unveiling under the heavy stares of the patrons and the barmaid, who all stayed silent. The Camford Arms was one of those not-too-popular suburban establishments surviving solely due to a handful of constant customers who spent half of their lives there. Any newcomer in such an 'exclusive' environment was usually met with open hostility.

In a minute or so, the silence was broken by a podgy little man known as Lionel the Loony.

"Look at them f…ing clones!" he uttered from his bar stool. And added: "Or is it me having a f…ing double vision?"

"I told you not to have that last pint, Lionel!" laughed Porky Pete – a barrel-shaped character with a mane of tousled ginger hair. "They are not f…ing clones, but f…ing twins!"

"No matter!" said Lionel. "Twins or clones – who cares. That lassie is quite a looker though," he beckoned at Catherine. "I would give it to her any time…"

"How about the other one? Not much of a difference, eh?" cackled Pete pointing his hairy sausage-like finger at Katherine.

"Yeah, I'd give it to her too, but only if she asks me nicely!"

"What did you say, you creep?" Viktor came up to Loony's bar stool and grabbed him by the shirt collar.

"Don't touch me, you posh wanker! Go and grope your f…ing twin whores instead!" Lionel pushed Viktor away with both hands.

"Hey, boys, no fighting here!" the barmaid mumbled semi-audibly from behind the bar without looking up.

It was now Victor's turn to react. But after his morning confrontation with Viktor which only led to shame and self-harm, he did not feel like fighting and remained silent. He just stood there and looked down at the floor.

"Not sure about you, but I've had enough of these bullies," Katherine whispered to Catherine.

"I agree. Our men, as always, are useless, so we must take control of the situation," she said and added: "If you and I are indeed the variations of one and the same person, you should have some martial arts experience too."

"A black belt in taekwonshu," Katherine smiled. "How about you?"

"Well, in my case, it is only a red belt in kung chi, but I am still training for the black one," Catherine shrugged. "All female staff at our hospital have to attend a self-defence course."

"It's good we are both wearing jeans and can therefore do proper kicks. You take the fatty – and I'll deal with the ginger."

"What are you sluts whispering over there?" Porky Pete droned drunkenly. "Arguing as to who will service me first? Don't you worry: I can take both of you in one go."

From that moment on, everything went in fast motion. Katherine leapt towards Porky Pete, did a lightning-like turning kick in front of him, with her right foot hitting his chest. She could have kicked him in the face, but that was not necessary: Pete was already sprawled on the floor gasping for breath, like a large fat carp on a river bank.

At the same time, Catherine threw Lionel off his bar stool with a not-too-strong push kick. Loony stood up and tried to punch the woman, but she expertly blocked his hand with her right elbow and sent him flying with a brief, yet powerful, upper hook under his chin. Lionel hit the floor and lay motionless

The remaining patrons were watching the scene in consternation from their barstools and made no attempts to intervene.

A round of applause from Victor and Viktor followed.

"Well done, girls!" they shouted in chorus.

"It was your job!" said Catherine breathing heavily and pointing at the men.

"And your fault!" Katherine added. "Whichever of you two wanted a bloody pint."

"Ok, ok, guilty as charged," agreed Viktor. "Women are always right, don't we all know that? But now let's get out of here before these loonies call the police."

"Too late, you wankers!" the barmaid squealed from behind the till. "The police are on their way and will be here any second. You can't be allowed to maim my peaceful customers!"

"Let's run!" Catherine exclaimed.

But it was too late indeed. Out in the street, they nearly bumped into two burly policemen in full uniform getting out of a white Ford Montego, parked at the pub entrance, its blue lights blinking. The word "**Polise**" was painted in large black letters along the side of the car and on its roof too. Viktor was about to comment on another disgraceful spelling mistake, but his wife covered his mouth with her palm.

"Not a word, Vitya!" she said firmly. "Not now!"

Chapter Eleven

Improbable Probabilities

"Let us now consider the seemingly straightforward, yet, in actual fact, rather confusing issues of the likelihood, or probability, if you'd prefer a more conventional term."

Daniel Spiegeltent, Blumian Professor of Mathematics and Astronomy at the University of Camford, paused and looked up at the last and uppermost row of the University's main lecture theatre. It was one of his famous eccentricities – to pick one person in that row and maintain eye contact with him or her throughout the lecture. That habit of his was well known to students of the Applied Mathematics Department. On numerous occasions, they had tried to play a prank on the respected Professor by placing the year's prettiest girl in his line of vision and encouraging her to wink at him provocatively, her eyes blazing with simulated passion, hoping to take him off course. Bets were made on whether and how soon the venerable academic would get distracted and start confusing his words. Those bets had so far remained unclaimed: no amount of flirting seemed to be able to confound their acclaimed lecturer – the fact that initially led to heated debates about the Professor's sexual orientation. But substituting – for the sake of experiment, no doubt – a pretty girl with a no less handsome young male student had achieved the same results, i.e. absolutely nothing. Indeed, it seemed that no force on the planet was capable of interrupting Spiegeltent's impeccable line of thinking and undermining the iron logic of his carefully balanced and clearly articulated pronouncements. Eventually, the pranksters had to give up and the Professor could allow himself to get fully immersed in his fascinating (from his point of view) subject – the Probability Theory.

"There are many problems, such as those of games of chance, where the hypothesis is trusted to such an extent that the amount of observational material that would induce us to modify it would be far larger that will be available in any actual trial," he carried on, oblivious to the fact that most of the students in the theatre were openly browsing the Lace on their mobile phones, and the good-looking young woman in the last row at whom he had been staring unseeingly was stretching her cute little mouth in a wide lioness-style yawn.

"We may still, however, want to predict the result of such a game. Let us, for example, take a bridge player, who may be interested to find out if – given that he and his partner have nine trumps between them – the remaining four trump cards are divided two and two. Here we have a pure matter of inference from the hypothesis to the probability of different events. Such problems are not new, and I shall have little to say about them, beyond indicating their general position in the theory…"

Daniel Spiegeltent loved his subject and wished at times he were able to express it in a clearer and much more literary way. He had always aspired to write thrillers and science fiction novels as opposed to his regular contributions to specialised mathematical journals, with more equations and formulas than words. But being a mathematician, not a writer, he lacked literary ability and had to stick to dry formulaic language.

Had he been a writer, not a scientist, he would probably limit the day's lecture to saying something like this: "No one can predict anything with certainty, but we can at least try to understand what certainty as such is about. The concept of probability is connected with many different events leading to many different results. By thinking logically about those various outcomes, we can make better decisions about our future and come to understand our present lives better too. We could also learn to cope with the general unpredictability of our existence and, who knows, perhaps even come to enjoy life's big and little uncertainties."

Or even more simply: "Don't panic when flying abroad, or just crossing a busy road. Just remember the statistics which make it clear that the probability of a fatal accident or even a minor injury is minuscule – one out of many millions – and virtually non-existent. Mind you, all statistics become meaningless, if YOU yourself happen to belong to that luckless minuscule minority who found themselves in the proverbial wrong place at the no-less-proverbial wrong time."

Unlike the Probability Theory he was teaching, Spiegeltent's own life was very predictable. A top student of his year, he stayed at his own *alma mater* to do his post-graduate degree and was then promptly offered a teaching job in another university, not far from London. He soon married one of his fellow teachers, with whom they eventually had two kids – a boy and a girl, both grown up and living in London now. He and his wife did not like travelling and only went abroad once a year, for a traditional beach holiday in Halkidiki, Greece. This kind of existence was not what he imagined for himself in his youth. He wanted a life full of adventures and, yes, uncertainties, for what is an adventure? It is something if not always extraordinary, then definitely out of the ordinary; something that goes against daily routine – the biggest enemy of hope and promise. In his memories, Spiegeltent often looked back at his last encounter with his friend Peter Burgess, now a police Superintendent, but then just a tyro constable, well over twenty years ago. He often thought of the mysterious Man from Tavrida: his amazing hotel registration form and his inexplicable disappearance. Did he indeed arrive from a different world – a kind of alternative universe? If so, Spiegeltent would give ten years of his life to take a peek at that hidden dimension, where he could be enjoying a totally different and a much more eventful life, full of surprises and unexpected happenings. Shortly after the incident, he even asked his colleagues from the Department of Engineering to develop and manufacture a special infra-red quantum scanner, with the help of which he was hoping to explore the interior of the Travel Inn, where the Man from Tavrida disappeared from, for the existence of a portal to a different dimension. The scanner was duly made and presented to Spiegeltent as a slightly eccentric gift for his thirtieth birthday, but up to the present moment, the Professor himself had not been able to find time to carry out the investigation, and the engraved scanner was gathering dust in one of his desk drawers…

"Where was I?" he asked the students.

"You were talking about statistics," said a big-eyed young woman in the front row – the only person in the auditorium who seemed to be actually listening to what he was saying and even making notes – in round childish handwriting – in a neat pink notebook in front of her.

"What a pretty girl!" Spiegeltent thought ruefully. "I must look ancient to her. But in an alternative world, who knows, I could probably be her father, her elder brother or even her boyfriend, why not?"

"Yes, statistics," he said trying to look the girl straight in the eye. "Statistics are stubborn, as they say in Russia. Stubborn and persistent, I can add…"

At that very moment, the curly head of Jane, a departmental assistant, peered through the auditorium door.

"An urgent phone call for you, Sir! Sorry for interrupting."

"Can't they wait? I am in the middle of a lecture!" Spiegeltent frowned.

"I am afraid they can't. There is an extreme urgency to this call," Jane insisted.

"OK. Do some revision! I will be back shortly" he told the students, all of whom suddenly – for the first time since the start of the lecture – got excited and were talking loudly to each other. It was clear that revision would be far from their agenda in the Professor's absence.

The moment Spiegeltent was out of the auditorium, Jane handed him her mobile phone. He pressed it to his ear and heard the voice of his old friend Peter Burgess: "Daniel, how are you, mate? I am actually calling from the office. It's a bit of an emergency, I am afraid, and your presence is needed. Could you please make your way to the police station immediately? Our patrol car is waiting outside."

Superintendent Burgess himself met Professor Spiegeltent at the entrance to Camford Police Station. They embraced.

After a brief exchange of pleasantries of the "long-time-no-see" type and regulation enquiries about each other's health and families, Burgess escorted his old friend to a second-floor interview room.

"We need your assistance in this rather delicate matter," the policeman was saying as they were walking up the stairs. "But please, Daniel, promise that you'll keep everything you see and hear to yourself."

"Just like twenty-five years ago?" asked Spiegeltent, secretly rejoicing at the prospect of adding yet another unpredictable adventure to his highly probable scientific life.

"Yes, just like then," the policeman smiled.

From Professor Daniel Spiegeltent's Dossier:

As these truly incredible events keep unfolding, I decided to start a dossier in which I will try to record them with maximum accuracy and precision. Well, to be honest, it is going to be more of a diary than a dossier, because certain facts, particularly as puzzling and mind-boggling as the ones I had to face, the facts, which, despite being triggered by complex scientific phenomena, seem to be firmly rooted in normal everyday life, are better recounted by way of literary narrative than by dry scholastic reporting.

When the tedious routine of my daily existence was suddenly interrupted by my old friend Peter Burgess, I did not and could not immediately realise the enormous effect they were going to have on my life and career. But let me first come back to that scorching summer afternoon when I was urgently summoned to the police station.

On entering the second-floor interview room after Peter, I saw two men and two women sitting around a crude old wooden table covered with stains and cigarette burns. One glance at them was enough to realise that they were couples. The next thing that struck me was that both men and both women looked like twins, despite differences in hairstyles and clothing. Yet, somehow, from the way they looked at each other, it was clear that they were not siblings.

I forgot the name of the author who said that until a writer describes his fictional characters' clothes, they (the characters) appear naked to the reader. Well, I am not a writer (maybe one day I will be), and my 'characters' are not at all fictional, but I think I should mention here what they were wearing – not for the sake of some hypothetical 'reader', but for the convenience of my own research: any distinctive feature is helpful when talking about twins, or close lookalikes, if you wish.

Both women were wearing similarly cut pink T-shirts and jeans of the same brand (I was never too good with recognising popular labels), but of different colours: black and navy. One woman's T-shirt had a logo, "I hate people" across the chest. The men were both sporting beige cotton trousers, but whereas one was wearing a simple black T-shirt, the other was clad in a sky-blue turtleneck. At first glance, it was hard to determine who was attached to whom, but it was obvious that they all were not strangers and knew each other well.

As I have said already, all four of them were sitting – rather uncomfortably, it seemed – at the table, which had all four legs screwed to the floor – a common feature of the scarce furniture pieces in prisons and police stations. Towering above them all was a tall young man in the uniform of Police Sergeant.

When Peter and I entered, he stopped pacing about the room and introduced himself as Sergeant Nick Draper.

Here it needs to be said that I am describing the scene in such detail to make it easier for me or for anyone who may happen to read this dossier in the future to reconstruct all the extraordinary circumstances with ultimate precision.

"This is my old friend and colleague Professor Daniel Spiegeltent," said Peter Burgess, addressing not the Sergeant, but the two couples at the table. "He may be just the person you said to me you were looking for," he added.

"Thank you, Sir. Can we go now?" asked one of the men without looking up at us.

"Not yet, not yet!" said Sergeant Draper. "Not before we find out all the circumstances behind the serious offence you have committed."

"We told you already, Sergeant, that we were simply trying to protect ourselves from being abused by those foul-mouthed bullies in the pub," said the woman wearing the "I hate people" T-Shirt.

"To protect?" Sergeant chuckled. "You have inflicted serious bodily harm on two unsuspecting pub patrons, who, incidentally, did not even touch you. To me, it doesn't look like reasonable self-defence, but rather some rampant and violent vigilantism! You guys do really 'hate people', don't you?" he barked out pointing at the woman's T-shirt logo.

"Whoa, Sergeant, wait a moment," interrupted Peter. "I agree they might have overdone it a bit, but 'violent vigilantism' sounds a tad too harsh. What would you do if your wife or girlfriend were showered with horrible obscenities in full view of the public? Would you feel like swallowing it all and calling the police? Or would you be more likely to momentarily lose control and protect your woman from the abuse on an impulse?"

"That's the whole point, Sir: as I have just established while you were out of the room meeting your friend, it was not the men but the ladies here who did all the fighting!"

"Did they really?" Superintendent Burgess looked genuinely surprised.

"Yes, it was us," nodded the woman in a logo-less T-shirt. "It's just that we... I mean Katherine and I happen to be practising martial arts in our free time, and our husbands are both very peaceful gentlemen who don't know how to fight. So we... Katherine and I... just decided to take matters into our own hands, so to speak, to show that we are capable of protecting ourselves."

"You sure are!" Sergeant Draper noted sarcastically. "A broken nose, a twisted ankle and a couple of dislocated joints – all within seconds. Good job, ladies!"

"Let's put the fight aside for a moment," said Peter. "I want to raise another interesting issue. The names you gave the Sergeant on detention – first and last – all sound very similar. Just minor spelling differences. What's even more fascinating is that none of them seem to feature in either police database or election rolls. The closest match we could find was one local married couple with a slightly different last name, but, sadly, they both perished in a car crash the other day. Can you please explain who you are and where you have come from?"

"Let me try and explain," the man in the black T-shirt stood up, like a schoolboy in front of a teacher. He spoke with a slight East European accent.

"I happen to be a technology journalist," he said looking straight in front of himself. "That is why I am familiar with some of the latest developments in the fields of particle physics, cosmology and quantum mechanics. As you may have heard, the scientists working on the fringes of those three disciplines have recently come up with the theory of multiple universes, or the multiverse theory, as it is often called."

"We don't need a lecture in popular science," interrupted Sergeant Draper. "Professor Spiegeltent here, I am sure, knows more about the theories you've mentioned than all of us taken together. Am I right, Professor?"

I felt embarrassed and muttered something to the effect that the multiverse theory was still not much more than a hypothesis – a strong one, but still a hypothesis…

"Carry on, Mr Petrov," said Peter Burgess. "And could I ask you, Sergeant, to kindly leave the room? You were not meant to question the detainees anyway – just to note their names and addresses and take their fingerprints, remember?"

"As you say, Sir!" Sergeant Draper shrugged and went out.

"May I continue?" The man in the black T-shirt seemed to have regained his composure. "Shortly after my wife and I returned from Majorca the other day, we started noticing little discrepancies in the all too familiar environment, some small deviations from how we used to know it."

"What kind of discrepancies?" asked Peter Burgess. "Can you be more specific please?"

"Initially, we noticed some little things like spelling mistakes in road signs and so on."

"Can you give an example?"

"Yes. We noticed that the ambulance that gave us a lift home after the car crash on the way from the airport carried the word 'ambulanse' – with an 's', not a 'c' – on its side, and on its roof too."

"So, what's wrong with that?" enquired Peter. "Every schoolkid knows that the only correct way to spell 'ambulanse' is with an 's', not with a 'c' at the end."

"But this is the whole point!" The man exclaimed. "When we left the country a couple of weeks earlier, the word 'ambulance' and lots of other everyday words used to be spelled differently!"

"Like 'police' which used be spelled with a 'c', not an 's'!" the other man added from his seat pointing at the wall poster behind his back. "**Polise Notise. Do not Comit Crime**", it ran.

It was now my turn to intervene.

"Let's forget about the spelling variations for a moment," I said. "After all, we all make mistakes every now and then. You mentioned the car crash you were in on the way from the airport. Those discrepancies, as you called them, did you start noticing them before or after the crash?"

The man rubbed his forehead.

"Not sure, Sir… I cannot recall anything unusual inside the airport…"

"And I can!" said the turtleneck man. "Starting with the airport sign – that had an extra 'a' in it and read 'Stanstead' instead of 'Stansted'!"

"But that is correct too!" Peter Burgess exclaimed. "Same as 'Highstead' or 'homestead' – it all makes sense. What are you trying to say here?"

"Wait a moment," I had to intervene again. "Did you all arrive back in the UK on the same day?"

"Yes, Sir. My wife and I returned from our traditional short holiday break in Majorca on the same day as that other couple."

"And you have also been to Majorca? Unbelievable…"

"Maybe, now can I carry on at last?" said the man in the black T-shirt sarcastically. "Thank you very much!"

"Stop clowning, Victor!" the slim and attractive lady in blue jeans (well, they were both slim and attractive!), probably Victor's wife, said suddenly. "Let me take the floor – and I will be quick and straightforward, just like during that disgusting pub incident. I don't know how on earth it has happened but it looks like both we and they – (she pointed at the other man and his wife across the table) have stumbled into an alternative world – the world of that other third couple who died in the car crash – where none of us four seem to belong."

That was a grossly implausible statement, I thought. It was one thing for the solitary Man from Tavrida to turn up in a different dimension before disappearing without a trace. But to have four people taking the same route… Totally impossible! Well, almost…

"You mean you and your husband and that couple sitting next to you have crossed into this world simultaneously?"

"Yes, simultaneously or almost simultaneously, and from two different universes too!"

"How about the third couple that perished? Had they arrived from yet another universe?" asked Peter Burgess.

"Can I at last open my mouth?" Victor was now so agitated he was nearly shouting. "The third couple had not arrived from anywhere, can't you understand? They had lived here, in this very universe, where all of us are now, and in that very cottage where we and our two... er... opposite numbers... ended up coincidentally on the very day they tragically lost their lives!"

"Coincidentally? To me that looks like the hell of a coincidence!" said Peter. He then turned to me: "What do you think, Daniel?"

"Coincidences are not that uncommon," I said. "But here, it seems, we are dealing with not just one, but a whole cluster of them. And according to the Multiverse Theory, the only limit to the number of different possibilities, or probabilities, or coincidences, if you wish, is human imagination, for, if that theory is correct, whatever can be imagined is possible. Can we then imagine, even if just in theory so far, that the dwellers of the cottage could die in a car crash on the same day that their counterparts from two different universes, who had all undergone a kind of a shake-up, be it air turbulence or a relatively minor road accident, find their way into the first couple's universe and into their cottage too? Well, I am talking about it and you are all listening to me which means we do not immediately exclude the possibility of that happening – and this in itself is enough to make it all probable, at least theoretically so."

"Wait a moment, Daniel," interrupted Peter. "With all due respect, if what you are saying is true and I am now going to assume that not just two couples from two different universes but twenty thousand other people from the same number of different worlds have all crossed over and are now wandering somewhere in the outskirts of Camford starting fights in local pubs, it makes it all plausible, possible and hence real too?"

"This is where the probability theory kicks in, Peter," I replied to my friend. "What we have here, in your twenty-thousand-people scenario, is the so-called phenomenon of errors of observation, defined by Laplace and Gauss. The impossibility of exact multiple prediction has been forced on us by Heisenberg's Uncertainty Principle. Sorry if all this sounds too esoteric. Heisenberg considered the most refined and the most unlikely types of observation possible to obtain a lower and a higher limit to the uncertainty. Your twenty-thousand assumption by far exceeds those limits which makes it all extremely unlikely, with a probability ratio of one to trillions of trillions of trillions…"

At this point, the other young woman (not the one in the "I hate people" T-shirt) stood up from the table and looked at me pleadingly with her wide open warm green eyes.

"Dear Professor!" she said. "We don't care about all those theories and numbers. We are real and we are here. Help us, please! Help us get back home, to our normal worlds!"

Chapter Twelve

Probable Improbabilities

Throughout the questioning of two twin couples, Superintendent Peter Burgess had been tempted to take the peculiar 'Concise Atlas of the World' out of his pocket to ask the couples if it belonged to them and, if yes, then how and where they had acquired it. Not only could that throw plenty of light on the so far mysterious connection between them and the Man from Tavrida, but it could also provide a clue to the whereabouts of an alternative universe portal, which the couples – without realising it – could have used. The only reason he didn't do it was the fact that he had broken into the couples' cottage on an impulse and had searched the premises and the dwellers' personal belongings without a warrant. An experienced policeman, Burgess knew only too well that his actions constituted not just a breach of rules, but a serious offence, and could significantly impede any future investigation and even ruin a criminal case, if any. If raised in court, that issue could also signify the end of his so far thriving police career.

It was now obvious to Burgess that the two couples (or just one couple which has doubled – no matter) had so far been innocent of any wrongdoings in the pub, for they were acting purely in self-defence, under a serious threat of violence, and he therefore had to let them go shortly. He also realised that he had to get to their cottage before them – to put the Atlas back into the suitcase where he had found it, and to tidy up the bedrooms and the lounge to conceal the signs of his intrusion. He therefore had to try and delay the moment of the couples' release and find an excuse to disappear for an hour or so.

"Apologies, but can I have a quick word with Professor Spiegeltent in private?" he said.

Burgess led his friend to the farthest corner of the dark and empty police station corridor, showed him the Atlas and explained how he found it.

"This is amazing!" Spiegeltent exclaimed gleefully looking at the map with Tavrida on it.

"Yes, it is!" said Burgess. "All four of them have just returned from Majorca and the Man from Tavrida had been there too. We must somehow lure the couples, or at least one of them, back to Palma, preferably to the same place where they had stayed, and watch them closely. If there's an explanation to all this, it must be there – and they will lead us to it!"

"I agree," Spiegeltent nodded.

"Brilliant! So while I am replacing the book and tidying up the cottage, could you please stay here with them and keep the conversation going? They must never find out that I actually rummaged through their luggage."

"Don't you worry, Peter. I think I know how to keep them interested for at least an hour," Spiegeltent promised. "Believe it or not, but I was myself thinking of sending them back to Majorca – for a very different reason though."

"That's interesting," said Burgess. "Let's go back to the interview room, but before we do so, let me quickly pop into our forensic laboratory. I'll be back with you in a tick."

In less than two minutes, Burgess re-joined his old friend in the corridor. He looked pale and – just like all those years ago in the pub – he was stuttering with excitement.

"D-daniel, you won't believe it, but I've just checked the fingerprints we took of the couples. They are identical for both males and for both females too! Moreover, in both cases, they are exactly the same as those of the third couple that perished in the car accident yesterday!"

"This is extraordinary!" Spiegeltent exclaimed.

"Yes, Daniel. Please, not a word about it to the couples themselves. Not yet."

They hurried back to the interview room.

"I am sorry, but a serious crime has just been committed in central Camford and I have to inspect the scene," Burgess announced to the Cs and the Ks. "I will be back in about one hour, and in the meantime, Professor Spiegeltent will keep you company. You were asking for help with getting back to where you have come from – and he may be just the person you need."

Having run downstairs to the station's basement garage, Burgess commandeered the first available police car and drove away.

After Superintendent Burgess's sudden departure, silence reigned inside the interview room for several long minutes. The Petrovs and the Petroffs were staring at Professor Spiegeltent across the table – and he was staring back at them, without saying a word. The pause was finally broken by Viktor.

"Excuse me, Sir," he said to the Professor, "but your policeman friend said before leaving that you might be just the person who could help us return to our respective universes. Do you really think you can and if so, then how?"

The Professor was not in a hurry to respond. He kept looking Viktor straight in the eye, saying nothing.

At long last, when his silence started to feel awkward, he spoke.

"Yes, I may indeed be able to help you, but it could take a very long time, and your complete understanding and co-operation will be required. Plus you will all have to sign a written statement to protect me against any repercussions in case my attempts fail."

"We will sign anything, Professor!" said Catherine. "What have we got to lose anyway?"

"Yes, we are so very lucky to have found you!" added Katherine with a seductive half-smile. And although the smile was aimed at the Professor and not at him, it made Victor's heart miss a beat.

"Could you please explain what exactly you have in mind?" he asked.

As a journalist, Victor was familiar with one of the basic rules of interviewing: try and keep the subject as close to the heart of the matter as possible without letting the interviewee beat about the bush for too long.

"I will certainly try," the Professor replied. "The lovely lady opposite me may be right: you are indeed very lucky to have met me. And I am saying this not as an egomaniac, but as this country's and, possibly, this planet's biggest authority on the theory of probability."

"Wait a second, Professor," interrupted Viktor. "But what has that theory to do with us? I would think we'd actually need an expert in quantum physics, astronomy or cosmology…"

"And you are wrong, young man!" the Professor retorted. "Incidentally, alongside the theory of probability, I also teach courses in applied mathematics, quantum mechanics and cosmology too. But it is the probability theory that has more do with your… er… predicament than any of the above."

An experienced lecturer and public speaker, Professor Spiegeltent paused again. He carried on only when he knew he had the couples' complete and undivided attention.

"Let me try and explain it to you in simple terms. We mathematicians are not dreamers. We are realists trying to apply logic and reason to solve life's most incredible mysteries. Any unlikely happening that may seem like a case of providence, miracle or coincidence to you is actually regulated by the laws of probability. Could you please give me an example of the most bizarre and unlikely occurrence you can think of?"

"Winning a lottery jackpot twice in a row?" Catherine suggested meekly.

"Or how about being repeatedly struck by lightning?" suggested Viktor.

"Excellent!" the Professor was clearly enjoying himself. "But you all know of course that both of those highly improbable scenarios have actually happened in reality – and not once! And here mathematics and quantum theory come together to state that anything, absolutely anything outside sheer physical impossibility that one can imagine happening, will happen eventually. It is just the question of when…"

"Wait a moment, Professor!" It was now Victor's turn to interrupt. "Like most writers, even if technology ones, I have a rich imagination and can easily imagine a snowstorm happening in the middle of the Harasa desert in summer. If we are to believe what you've just said, it is only the question of when it will occur…"

"You have missed one important point, young man," said Spiegeltent. "I said 'anything you can imagine outside physical impossibility', remember? I am not familiar with that particular desert you've mentioned, but a snowstorm in any kind of arid desert, just like a fifty-degree heatwave at the North Pole, are natural impossibilities with zero probability of happening. As the great Russian writer Chelstoy said jokingly: 'It cannot happen, because it can never happen!' Or, in the words of the no-less-great British author, Sir Arthur Donan-Coyle, who, incidentally, was also a doctor and hence a scientist of sorts: 'Once you eliminate the impossible, whatever remains, no matter how improbable, must be the truth.'"

He paused again waiting for another question but none came.

"Here we come to the crucial issue of the odds, or likelihood," he continued. "What would be the likelihood of a card player being served all thirteen diamonds in one game? The odds for or rather against such a scenario have been calculated as (he scribbled the twelve-digit number on a piece of paper and showed it to the couples) 635,013,559,600 to 1 – about the same as being struck by a meteorite one second after being hit by lightning. But does it mean that either of above scenarios is as impossible as a heavy snowstorm in the desert in summer? Not at all. Mathematicians have even invented a formula for the probability of something extraordinary happening or not happening, the so-called Bayes' Theorem, formulated by the eighteenth century English statistician and priest Thomas Bayes. But I won't bother you with that."

The Petrovs and the Petroffs were listening to the Professor without interrupting.

"So let's consider a far less unlikely probability. Do you know, for example, that it only takes the presence of twenty-three different people in one room for a fifty percent probability that two of them will share the same birthday?"

"Ha! There are four of us here – five if we count you, Professor – but both our wives share the same birthday, and so do Viktor and I!" exclaimed Victor.

"I was expecting you to say that," Professor Spiegeltent smiled. "In fact, I gave that last example deliberately to check one little theory of mine."

"What kind of theory?" wondered Viktor.

"The theory about you people. I have reason to believe that, apart from the old me, there are not four people in this room, but just two!"

"How come?" all four (or perhaps just all two?) exclaimed in chorus.

"Well, if you all have indeed strayed into this world from two alternative universes, then the two ladies and the two gents here are in fact just one lady and one gentleman in two incarnations each. That is why it helps to make sure that both men – as well as both women – share the same birthday. I can now also bet you that it is not just the days and the months that are shared here, but the years of birth too!"

"Yes, you are right, Professor," said Katherine. "We established that the moment we all started talking. Indeed, Catherine and I were born on exactly the same day, month and year, and so were our husbands."

"But the dates of our marriages are not the same!" Catherine intervened.

"This doesn't surprise me at all," said Spiegeltent. "The truth is that if you do come from two parallel universes, you are bound to be very much alike, and yet – slightly different, for had you been exactly the same, you would still inhabit one and the same world!"

"Sorry, Professor, I find it very hard to grasp," said Catherine with her eyes closed. "Just thinking of it all gives me a headache. Can we please forget about theories and maths and come back to the practicalities: how – or whether – we can return to where we came from?"

"This is exactly where we are heading for, young lady! But probabilities do not exist in some kind of vacuum; they are all dependant on a number of circumstances. According to Thomas Bayes, the probability of an event is based on conditions related to that event. By creating – or rather recreating – the conditions of an initial happening, or an event, we are increasing the probability of it happening again! Do you now understand what I am hinting at?"

All four (or was it just two?) shook their heads.

Superintendent Burgess took the Atlas out of his pocket and carefully placed it inside the suitcase he had taken it from several hours before. On the way to the cottage, he stopped at a newsagent and photocopied parts of the book, including the title page and the map with Tavrida on it.

Having made sure that all three upstairs bedrooms looked pretty much as he found them earlier, he walked down to the lounge, which was in need of some tidying up too. There was plenty of time to do so, or so he thought…

The sudden sound of the doorbell made him shudder.

"Bloody hell! Who could this be?" Burgess's first instinct was to hide in the kitchen and not to react. He opened the kitchen door, but was greeted with an ear-piercing meowing and had to retreat.

"Koshkin, dear! Mummy is coming to get you!" an old woman's voice, with a strong East European accent, shouted from behind the front door, and Burgess realised that his cover had just been blown.

It should now be obvious to whoever was outside that there was someone else, and not just the cat, inside the cottage. "What if she thinks the place has been burgled and calls the police?" he thought. "That would be a perfect pickle." Being uncovered by his own colleagues and accused of an unlawful and unauthorised break-in would be his ultimate nightmare and the end of his police career. On the other hand, it was obvious to Burgess that he had to open the door – there was simply no other option.

He turned the handle and the door sprang ajar. Behind it stood a buxom elderly lady in a black widow's kerchief. In her hand, she was holding a large woven basket – empty apart from some fluffy blue rags covering its bottom.

"Why police?" she screamed in high-pitch falsetto upon seeing Burgess. "Are my children OK? Or have they done something naughty?"

"No worries, Ma'am, we are simply here answering a routine call."

"Call? Who called you? Must have been Vitya, my son! That wife of his, Kat'ka, is violent; yes, she is! She was probably hitting him again. And my boy will never hurt a fly, I can tell you."

"Whoa… wait a second, ma'am… No one was hitting anyone here. At least, we are not aware of any violence. It may have just been a hoax call of which we receive many."

"Why do you think it was a hoax?" the woman carried on.

"Because when we arrived, nobody answered the door, so we had to exercise a forced entry, but found no one in the house."

"No one? I came here in the morning, and my son Vitya was definitely in. Only he was behaving in a strange manner: did not want to recognise me and kept asking after his late father."

"Well, ma'am, why don't you come in, so that we can talk in peace?" asked Burgess.

"Of course I will come in! If only to check on Koshkin, my other baby. I heard him meowing – he must be hungry. They always forget to feed the little moggy."

"Are you talking about that huge black cat in the kitchen? I wouldn't call him a little moggy," mumbled Burgess, moving aside to let the woman in.

She ran inside with unexpected prowess and headed straight for the kitchen. It was obvious she had been in the house before and knew its layout. In no time, Burgess could hear her cooing to the cat: "Oh, my poor little baby… what have they done to you, those naughty Vit'ka and Kat'ka… Locked you in the kitchen… Forgot to give you food… Your mummy was worried about you, and she was right… I brought some food for you, darling…"

She emerged from the kitchen a couple of minutes later.

"I am taking my baby back! They simply cannot look after him properly!" she announced.

"Come and sit down for a moment," said Burgess, leading the way to the lounge. The woman – rather reluctantly – followed.

She perched herself on the edge of a chair uneasily, with her hands folded on her lap.

"Can you please introduce yourself?" asked the policeman.

"I am Elvira Petrovas, mother of Victor, and Kat'ka's mother-in-law!" she said with badly hidden challenge in her voice. "And who are you, if I may ask?"

"I am Peter Burgess, Superintendent, Camford Police Station." He showed the woman his police badge.

"So my children did not do anything naughty?" she asked.

"I've told you already: it was a hoax call, and I was about to leave the house when you arrived. Before I go, can I ask you something, ma'am? You said your family name was 'Petrovas', not 'Petrov'."

"Yes, this is my name! Has been for nearly forty years now, since I married Victor's father."

"So, Victor's father ceased?"

"He certainly did. Years ago. But Vitya sounded as if he had forgotten about it this morning. Can you please tell me where my children are and when they are going to come back?"

"I know no more than you do," Burgess shrugged. "As I said, I am about to go, and maybe you should leave too."

Well, he certainly did know more. From the protocol of yesterday's fatal car crash, he knew that the family name of the dead couple was Petrovas. The husband's mother, Elvira, must have turned up at the cottage this morning and mistaken Victor Petrov, or possibly Viktor Petroff, for her son.

"I am not going anywhere!" Elvira stated decisively. "I am staying here to wait for my boy and his wife to come back! Koshkin will keep me company!"

Burgess was at a loss. Now was the time to tell the old lady that her beloved 'boy' was killed in a road accident yesterday. But how could he? She would then recall seeing him this morning, hours after the fatal car crash. If he were to tell her the truth now, she would almost certainly follow the example of poor PC Hartley and go crazy. Or, taking into account her podginess and her venerable age, she could even have a heart attack and kick the bucket there and then... No, he simply could not take this kind of risk. He had to come up with a plausible lie, and ask one of the couples to return to the cottage posing as Elvira's dead "children". But only ONE couple! The other one had to disappear! For her at least. But where to? To Majorca?

"OK, you can stay here, if you wish," he sighed. "You must have been in the house before, so should know where the tea, sugar and biscuits are. Have a nice time!"

"And what if old Hugo turns up? Shall I let him in?"

"Hugo? Who is he?" Burgess, already on his way out, stopped and looked back at Elvira.

"He is Kat'ka's father. This morning he turned up here shortly after I did with a dog called either Shirak or Koresh, can't remember. The dog stayed here after he left."

"A dog? Whose dog?"

"No idea. But Hugo behaved like he thought the dog was Vitya's and Kat'ka's too. He must have lost his marbles completely, the old git."

"And where is this dog now?"

"How do I know? I hope Koshkin gave him a good thrashing and he ran away; he hates dogs, my little baby."

"It's getting madder and madder," Burgess thought ruefully. "As if Elvira is not enough, now we have an old man and a dog to worry about... Another reason why all four of them can never come back here."

He waved to Elvira and resolutely went towards the door. As he was getting into the car, he heard some loud barking from the cottage's back garden.

Chapter Thirteen

Noughts and Crosses

"To make it simple, let's look at it like this…" Professor Spiegeltent was saying to the Cs and the Ks sitting at the table in front of him in the police station's interview room.

"You are searching for a way home away from your home grounds. To find it, all you have to do is look at everything in reverse. Because naturally, if you are away from home and keep walking, you walk further away. To find home, you have to turn round and go back. Does it make sense to you?"

"Yes, Professor, I think I begin to understand your line of thinking," said Katherine. "You mean to say that to have a good chance of getting back to where we came from, we need to retrace our footsteps on the way here."

"Precisely! And the more strictly you stick to the exact pattern of your movements on the way here, the higher is the probability that the whole scenario gets reversed and you end up in the very world you've come from. Mind you, due to the sheer number of possibilities, that probability would still be extremely small, but it will certainly be higher than zero!"

"That sounds hopeful, Professor," commented Victor. "But up to what point do we have to retrace our routes?"

"A very relevant question, young man," Spiegeltent was enjoying himself greatly. He could not recall being so excited since the Man from Tavrida episode many years ago. "A very relevant question which means that before you can embark on your homecoming journey, each of you has to figure out very clearly at which point in time the interference of two universes – that mini-Big Bang of yours – occurred. Just like with the initial universe-forming Big Bang, that was likely to happen at the moment of some considerable shock, shake up, or even…"

"Air turbulence!" interrupted Viktor. "I am absolutely sure that in our case the interference occurred during that massive shake up of our plane on its way from Palma! It was shortly after that, on landing in Stansted, that I started spotting all those ridiculous spelling mistakes!"

"And in our case, it must have been the car accident!" exclaimed Victor. "Prior to it, I hadn't noticed anything unusual or untoward."

"Both of your guesses sound valid to me," said Spiegeltent. "That means that the air turbulence couple should return to Majorca and try to meticulously repeat all their actions, no matter how insignificant they may appear now, several days prior to the flight."

"I've got a diary of what we did: my food poisoning and so on," said Katherine.

"That should make it easier," Spiegeltent agreed.

"And how about us? Do we need to return to Majorka too?" asked Catherine.

"Well, in your case, I do not see a huge necessity of doing so immediately," Spiegeltent shrugged. "And the reasons for that are as follows. To begin with, a car crash is a much more powerful shake-up and shock for your bodies and minds than air turbulence, no matter how strong. Also, the fact that it occurred when you were already on UK soil, reduces the necessity to travel to Majorca even further. In your case, I would advise several careful recreations of your car accident. The more – the better. Theoretically, you could keep going on until it actually works, but that could take thousands of years. I would initially limit the number of attempts to ten and hope that one of them works. If not, you could then switch over to the flight scenario. For safety reasons, those re-enactments will have to be conducted under strict police supervision, of course. I am sure our friend Superintendent Burgess will be both able and willing to help you with those."

"But how about us?" enquired Viktor. "Not sure we have the budget for travelling back to Majorca, staying at the same hotels and having the same restaurant meals all over again. We still have our mortgage to pay. Besides, we both are due back at work tomorrow."

"Well, work should not be a problem. You do not even know whether your respective offices exist in our universe here. As for the money, I've got several thousand pounds left from my departmental research budget. The money must be spent by the end of this financial year, or else they will cut the sum in the future – that's how it works. And I cannot think of a better scientific application of those funds as long as you allow me to use the data from the experiment – be it successful or not – in my future articles for scientific journals, maybe even a book."

"Of course, we will, no problem, Professor!" exclaimed Viktor. "Does it mean that you'll have to travel to Majorca with us?"

"Well, I may have to. But because I had not been in the picture at all during your initial stay in Majorca, my presence there will always be very discreet, and I would only be contactable in case of a problem you may face, or when in need of advice."

Catherine stood up, came up to Spiegeltent and gave him a hug.

"We should bless our lucky stars, Professor, that we have met you!"

"And everyone should now thank me for insisting on having that pint!" smiled Victor.

"Please do not rush to thank me," Spiegeltent replied. "As I said already, the only thing I can promise you is a slightly increased probability. Nothing else. Look at it as a lottery draw to which you previously had no tickets, so your chance of winning the jackpot was zero, zilch. Now, you've got a hundred tickets per couple. Does it mean you will definitely win? Absolutely not, if we remember all those millions of tickets sold."

"True, but it's better to have a hundred tickets than none!" concluded Viktor. "Can we now get back to the cottage and start packing?"

Spiegeltent had no time to respond. The door of the interview room suddenly flew open to let in Superintendent Burgess – red-faced and breathing heavily.

"Daniel," he gasped. "Can I have another word in private with you?"

In the corridor, Burgess quickly explained the situation to his friend.

"They cannot return to the cottage – not all four of them!" he finished emphatically.

"So what do we do?" asked Spiegeltent.

"You must find an excuse to separate the couples from each other, at least temporarily.

"Well, perhaps I could try and persuade the air-turbulence couple to fly to Majorca immediately?"

"That would be super!" said Burgess. "But how are you going to do that?"

They retraced their steps to the interview room where the two couples were waiting impatiently.

"Viktor and Katherine, or the Ks, can I have your complete attention?" said Spiegeltent. "I am sorry for the rush, but we, I mean you two and I, will have to fly to Majorca straight away. And remember: on the plane, you'll have to jot down your exact movements, minute by minute, during the last week, or at least three to four days on the island, and try to repeat each of them."

"What? We won't be able to go home and pick up our travel bags at least?" asked Viktor.

"No, your luggage will be delivered straight to the airport – our police friends will help you there."

He threw a furtive look at Burgess, who nodded in agreement.

"This rush is simply because, due to the position of the stars, now is the right moment to start looking for your way back home. I could tell you more, but that would be pure mathematics. What I am saying is that if you want an even bigger chance to get home, you must start here and now!"

Spiegeltent was not sure if his impromptu and rather far-fetched "position of the stars" explanation was going to work. But it did.

"I don't care about the luggage," said Katherine. "If we are going to get a better chance by starting now, so be it!"

Burgess looked up from the screen of his smartphone. "I've just checked with the Lace," he announced. "The next flight to Palma is leaving in two and a half hours."

The Ks stood up and, followed by Spiegeltent, started walking towards the door.

"We'll miss you!" the Cs yelled after them in chorus.

"We'll miss you too!" the Ks echoed.

"If we are not in luck, we'll meet again!" said Catherine looking more at Viktor than at Katherine.

"In which case – good luck to all four of us!" shouted Victor looking more at Katherine than at Viktor.

"You mean, to all two of us," the latter hurried to clarify.

"You still have time to give each other a hug," Burgess said benignly.

A very moving scene followed. Katherine and Victor immediately got locked in a tight embrace. Catherine and Viktor followed their example.

Looking at these diagonal farewells, Spiegeltent was reminded of his favourite childhood game of noughts and crosses. Suddenly he felt his eyes fill up with tears.

"Please calm down," he mumbled. "The whole scheme may not work, after all."

Chapter Fourteen

Repetitions and Returns

From Katherine's Diary:

At long last, I've found a moment to record the events of the last couple of days. Just like the previous ones, they were truly extraordinary.

After we said goodbye (or hopefully it was farewell) to our lookalikes and near-namesakes Victor and Catherine, a police car whisked us – Viktor, myself and Professor Spiegeltent – straight to the airport. At the same time, the police Superintendent, who had been in charge of questioning all four of us, took Victor and Catherine back to the cottage, from where he promised to come straight to the airport, having picked up our luggage. I asked him specifically to look out for the notebook with my diary which I left on the bedside table in our bedroom. That diary had suddenly acquired extreme significance, for on Professor Spiegeltent's advice, while back in Majorca, we will be expected to stick as closely as possible to what we did during the last days of our previous visit.

On the way to the airport, we briefly stopped at the university to allow Professor Spiegeltent to pop into his office, from where he recovered five thousand pounds – the remains of his research budget for the year. He gave some of the money to us and urged us to keep detailed records of all our expenses. The sum we received appeared sufficient enough to cover all our needs, for we were hoping not to spend more than five or six days on the island before flying off – back to our proper home, in the best of scenarios, or back to the cottage to re-join Victor and Catherine, in the worst (although, speaking frankly, the thought of a reunion with Victor in particular, did not appear so awful to me).

Two economy-class tickets to Palma, booked in our names by the police station's duty officer, were waiting for us at the ticket desk. To collect them, we needed our passports, and those – together with the rest of our travel accessories – were promptly delivered to us by Superintendent Burgess.

As for the Professor, he said that he had to complete some paperwork at the university, but would be flying to Majorca the following morning, and would supervise our progress there without staying in direct contact with us, for he did not want to interfere with our routine and thus jeopardise the success of our mission. He made sure, however, that, in case of an emergency, we could find him on the island easily and gave Victor a bespoke mobile phone to contact him. We gave it a test to make sure that, unlike the old mobiles we had brought with us, this one was in good working order.

The flight to Palma was uneventful, with no air or other turbulence, not counting Viktor's *sotto voce* grumblings about the quality of food served on board, and the ubiquitous spelling mistakes in the inflight magazine.

Well, so far so good: we didn't need the turbulence on this occasion, but would certainly pray for it to happen on the way back.

On landing in Palma, just like a couple of weeks ago, we took a bus to Port de Pollenca. By the time we reached it, it was already very late, so we decided to stay overnight at the Sis Pins, the same hotel we had spent a week at recently. Luckily, they had 'our' sea-view room vacant. And although we were not planning to start retracing our footsteps until the following morning, we thought it wouldn't do our mission any harm if we began somewhat earlier.

The sea view was of course irrelevant at that late hour, but all through the night we could hear the soothing sounds of the surf very clearly behind our room windows.

Before going to sleep, I consulted my diary notes, according to which we took a 6.05 am bus to Palma on the morning of our departure.

"Be ready for a very early start tomorrow," I said to Viktor.

"I will be, don't worry," he said and added: "I wish I were as sure as you seem to be that this whole scheme is going to work."

He sounded a bit down, and I could feel that he was missing Catherine. Well, to be absolutely honest, I myself couldn't stop thinking about Victor.

At exactly 6 am – with bags and baggage – we were waiting at a bus stop in the street, parallel to the promenade. The bus arrived on time and – just like on our previous journey – was about two-thirds full.

"Remember: the Professor said it was very important to try and recreate every minuscule detail. I think it would be good if we could travel in the same seats as last time, in row three on the left, behind the driver," I whispered to Viktor, having consulted my notes.

"Easier said than done," he responded with his favourite adage and with what I thought was some fiendish delight in his voice. "As you see, that row is occupied!"

Indeed, a very elderly couple in panama hats were sitting in state in those seats. From their clothes and the way they spoke, it was obvious that they were American. They seemed unmovable, but I thought I would try nevertheless.

"Excuse me, please," I said to the couple as the bus started moving. "Would you be so kind as to move to those two empty seats across the aisle? The reason is that my husband is mildly autistic and is also suffering from a rare kind of OCD. It is very important for him to sit in the row where you happen to be sitting."

From the look on my husband's face, I could see that he was about to protest and already opened his mouth to deny that he was autistic and had OCD, but then he remembered the Professor's advice and said nothing.

The elderly couple did not react and kept staring at the palm trees and vineyards flashing past the window. It was only then that I noticed the shrimp-like hearing aids sticking out of their ears.

I cleared my throat and shouted the same request at the top of my voice, at which point the little old lady, who was sitting near the aisle, turned her God's dandelion of a grey head to me and said in an unexpectedly hoarse and loud voice of a semi-deaf person: "I beg your pardon. What did you say, buddy? I couldn't hear a thing… These God damn hearing aids…"

I realised the futility of trying not just to move the old couple, but even of making them aware of what exactly we wanted and why.

"Never mind, ma'am!" I shouted. "Enjoy your journey!"

Viktor and I settled down in the very last row of the bus. It wasn't a good start to our homecoming endeavour. But there must be some justice in the world, after all: the old couple got off in Alcudia, and we were able to take over their – or shall I say 'our' – seats for the last hour of the journey, all the way to Palma.

While Viktor was nodding off in his seat, I studied the notes I had made during our previous visit. Our flight was due to depart at 7 pm, and it was not yet 9 am when the same coach from Port de Pollenca coughed us out in the centre of Palma. We then had a light breakfast of coffee and a piece of excessively sweet Gato d'Ametlla, Majorca's traditional almond cake (I have always been careful to record the names of dishes we ate abroad correctly, in case I would want to look them up later to cook at home) which we shared between the two of us, in a small café not far from the bus station. The café's owner was kind enough to agree to look after our baggage until 5 pm for just ten euros. I did not record the name of the coffee shop though, but thought we'd be able to recognise it anyway.

Having nearly seven hours to kill before we had to go to the airport, we then decided to temporarily split up, with me wishing to look at clothes shops and Viktor planning to visit some bookstores: it was his habit to check out bookshops in every town or city we visited when abroad, even if at times he didn't speak the local language. He said he simply liked looking at books. We agreed to meet up in Placa Major, the Main Square, at 1 pm and then go for lunch.

That particular meal of course gave me the massive food-poisoning which eventually was to delay our departure from Majorca by several days. With Professor Spiegeltent adamant in his demand that we should try and recreate every single thing that happened on that day, the thought of having to go through it all again did not sound particularly encouraging. But I decided to worry about it later.

Finding the café proved easy. It was called 'San Joan de S'Aigo'. The owner actually recognised us and asked why we were back in Majorca so soon. He must have recalled us picking up our suitcases on the way to the airport, with me in the throes of the food poisoning – feeling and looking more dead than alive. "We actually never left," Viktor was smart enough to reply. "We had to cancel our flights, and when my wife felt a bit better, headed to the north of the island, where we had spent several days."

"But tonight we will be flying away, you bet!" he added with a smile.

The owner seemed genuinely pleased to see us and offered to look after our luggage again, this time for free. Needless to say, it was an offer we were unable to refuse.

I spent several hours not so much browsing through shops, but having coffee and iced soft drinks outside different cafés, of which there was no shortage in central Palma. The bustling city's noisy and swarthy crowd was flowing past me, like a fast human river in which separate faces – just like separate ripples on the surface of the water – were impossible to discern. Or maybe it was me worried about the future and therefore unable to focus on anything or anyone. Palma has always struck me as an energiser, one of those Mediterranean cities which – due to their boundless energy, noise and smells – tend to appear much larger than they actually are. With the population of well under half a million, the relatively small Palma made an impression of a huge and bustling metropolis.

Viktor, clutching a couple of freshly acquired paperbacks, arrived to our meeting point in the Main Square at precisely 1 pm – he was always on time. I wondered if Victor was too. Don't know why but I was finding it hard not to think about the latter.

"More books!" I nagged him instead of greeting. "We haven't got an inch of extra space in our cottage to store them, have you forgotten?"

I immediately regretted my outburst: buying and owning, if not always reading, books had been Viktor's only hobby, one of the very few things in the world that seemed to make him happy.

"Which cottage do you mean?" he retorted. "The one where we spent the night before last had hardly any books at all."

"I mean our proper cottage... somewhere... wherever it can be..." I mumbled realising with sudden clarity how improbable and ridiculous our situation was.

"Let's not worry about it now," Victor said soothingly. "Look what else I've acquired in the bookshop called 'Babel' just round the corner."

Only then I noticed that he was holding a plastic bag, with something that looked like a bottle in it. And indeed, he dug into the bag and triumphantly produced a bottle of red wine. 'Macià Batle, 2013' said the label.

"You got this bottle in a bookshop?" I exclaimed.

"Indeed! It is the most amazing bookshop I've ever seen – full of all kinds of books, mostly fiction and mostly in Catalan and in Spanish, but it also sells local wines, with wine racks located straight under the bookshelves!"

"This is all very interesting, Vitya, but I don't recall you buying wine in a bookshop on our previous visit here."

"What do you mean?"

"I mean that by buying this bottle of wine you've deviated from what we did here last time – the routine we are supposed to stick to meticulously."

"Are you trying to say that by buying this bottle I've jeopardized the success of our mission?"

"I don't know, Vitya, but don't you remember what Professor Spiegeltent told us about trying to repeat all our movements and not to make any new ones?"

"Damn it, Katia. You must be right. I just got momentarily carried away in that amazing bookshop."

He stepped aside and put the bottle in a rubbish bin.

"Shame. I bought it to celebrate our potential home-coming."

"Never mind, Vitya. They have good wine in our universe too," I said and immediately wished I sounded more assertive and sure of myself.

We headed towards la Casa del Mar – the same seafood restaurant, where we had eaten lunch ten days ago.

"This restaurant used to pop up as the best seafood joint in Palma on the internet," Viktor noted as we were walking. "I wonder if it is the same on… what do they call it here… the World Wide Lace?"

"Who cares?" I replied.

Last time we sat inside the restaurant because of the air-conditioning, but today – by the time we arrived – all inside tables had been taken. We had to be happy with a small table for two on the vast restaurant's terrace, and I could only hope that the small discrepancy wouldn't affect the ultimate result of our complicated mission.

Just like ten days earlier, the menu had all kinds of fish – from locally caught *salmonete* (red mullet) to *cap roig*, or scorpion fish. Scared off by their not-too-appetising names, Majorcan or English, I was not tempted by either.

I suddenly felt very anxious. How on earth were we going to re-enact that fateful food poisoning – obviously an unforeseen and rare accident in this sterile-looking restaurant? And then – even if we somehow succeed, it will be me who would have to suffer all the consequences: high fever, nausea, vomiting, headache – all over again.

"Look," I said to my husband. "I know it's time for me to have the food poisoning, but – believe it or not – I don't have the slightest desire to go through that nightmare all over again. And in general, it looks like we are playing a losing game here. As the Professor himself insisted, the chances of us getting back to our universe are almost non-existent, so what's the point of all these trials? Why don't we just catch the first flight back to Stansted, or Stanstead, I don't care how it is spelled, and return to our cottage?"

"To share it with the Cs? Again?" he shrugged.

"Why not? I bet you wouldn't lose a chance to have another snog with Catherine. We could stay there for a couple of days and then find a new place for ourselves perhaps?"

"And how are we going to pay for that other place? All our money is in the blasted cottage, and I am not even sure if either, or any, of us is still employed in this strange universe. Besides, I will never feel at home in a country or a place where they spell 'Stansted' with 'ea' at the end, and 'police' and 'ambulance' with 's'. It will drive me mad very quickly."

"It won't be such a long drive, Vitya," I whispered .

"What did you say?" my husband cried out.

"Nothing. Let's just do it!"

"Easier said than done," he said (again). "I cannot just call a waiter and ask him to bring us some rotten food please, can I?"

"What are we going to do then?" I was beginning to feel desperate.

"When you don't know the answer – call a friend." Viktor took out his mobile phone. "Wasn't that what Professor Spiegeltent told us? He also encouraged us to feel free to call him any time if we get stuck. It is too noisy here, so I'll dial him from the loo which I was about to use anyway."

A waiter sporting a black vest, with a snow-white apron on top of it, came up to take our order.

"Can you please give us another five minutes?" asked Viktor.

Having consulted his notebook, in which the Professor had written down his number, he stood up from the table and went inside the restaurant.

From Catherine's Diary:

At long last, I've found a moment to record the events of the last couple of days. Just like the previous ones, they were truly extraordinary.

After our hasty farewells with the Ks at the police station, the policeman drove Victor and myself back to the cottage. I invited him to pop in for cup of tea, but he refused, saying he was very busy. The moment we got out of the car, he sped off, as if he was indeed in a hurry.

Loud low-pitched barking could be heard from our back garden.

"Looks like a neighbours' dog has strayed into our backyard," said Victor.

"Or could it be that oversize mongrel delivered by the old man this morning?" I suggested.

"Let me go and check," said my husband, opening the garden gate.

"Be careful, Vitya, the dog may have rabies!" I cried after him.

Then I unlocked the cottage's front door.

The moment I got inside, I could feel someone else's presence. And it was not just an old-fashioned woman's fur-coat (a bizarre thing to wear in the twenty-five-degree heat) on the hanger. It was that peculiar old lady's smell – of badly washed body and cheap perfume.

I was right. Elvira, that deranged East European hag, who had tried to pass herself off as Victor's late mother, was sitting in state on my precious Ligne Roset Togo lounge sofa, with Koshkin, or whatever the moggy's name was, on her knees. There were both asleep and snoring in unison.

A parquet floorboard squeaked under my feet – and Elvira woke up.

"Hey, Kat'ka," she addressed me without saying hello. "Where is my baby boy?"

"How… how… did you get in?" I stuttered.

"You must be out of your little mind, Kat'ka! You yourself gave me the keys before you and Viten'ka flew to Madeira and asked me to pop in once or twice during your absence to make sure everything was *khorosho*…"

"Oh, I am sorry, I must have forgotten," I said. "And we actually went to Majorca, not Madeira."

"Don't you argue with me, Kat'ka!" Elvira was getting angry. "Vitya said it was Madeira – and I am not mad, like you!"

At this point, the cat woke up too. Having jumped off Elvira's spacious lap, he stretched his back and walked up to me hissing threateningly.

I thought I'd rather change the subject.

"And where is Sharik, our dog?" I asked.

"Who? I never heard of a dog with such a stupid name. You know what it means in Russian? Little ball! Only a fool, with little balls, ha-ha, can call a pet that… But Kirash, old Hugo's mongrel, is running about the streets somewhere."

I gave up trying to make sense of anything she was saying. The woman had obviously lost all her marbles.

"Listen, ma'am," I said trying to remain calm. "You do look very much like my late mother-in-law, but this still doesn't explain your presence in my house. Nor does it give you the right to speak to me in that condescending and openly rude manner!"

At this point, Victor entered the room. He was dragging a huge Dalmatian on a strained leash. At the sight of the dog, Koshkin's eyes bulged and were sparking off like the ends of two short-circuited wires.

"Viten'ka!" with amazing dexterity for her age, Elvira jumped off the low Ligne Roset Togo sofa, which even Victor had always found hard to get off from, and dashed towards her son. Or rather towards my husband whom she was taking for her son.

"Viten'ka, Vitiusha, look at you! You are so thin – just skin and bones. Kat'ka must have been starving you! Never mind, my baby. Your mummy is now going to cook you a proper *oozhin*: your favourite *katleti* with buckwheat! Koshkin may enjoy them too, and as for Kat'ka, we are not going to give her any!"

Victor was staring at her with tears in his eyes. No wonder: seeing an exact double of one's late mother must be psychologically disturbing. His lips were moving, but no words came out. I started seriously fearing for his sanity. He also let go of the dog, who immediately pounced on Koshkin. Having tangled into one fluffy feline-canine ('fenine'?) ball, the animals rolled out of the room into the corridor. The scene did not appear to unnerve Elvira.

"I am off to the kitchen to make you a good *oozhin*!" she announced sombrely to Victor alone, as if I were an empty space and did not exist. "Will make an additional helping of *katleti*, in case old Hugo arrives soon!"

She was obviously fancying the poor old man, and I was sincerely hoping that – for his own sake – he never turned up.

The events were developing very quickly that evening. The moment Elvira disappeared into the kitchen, there came a peremptory knock at the door. To my relief, it was not Hugo, but a police constable from Camford, who, on Superintendent Burgess's orders, had delivered our car back to us.

"We've changed the tyre, checked the water and oil, so it all should be hunky-dory now," he smiled.

"How are you going to get back to Camford? Do you want a lift?" I asked him.

"No worries, ma'am, my colleague PC Dawson is waiting for me in a police car round the corner."

Superintendent Burgess seemed to have left no stone unturned.

"Some good news," I said to Victor back inside the cottage. He was now sitting on my beloved Ligne Roset Togo sofa, which he would normally try to avoid, on the same spot where his mo... sorry, Elvira had been sitting a minute ago, in a truly catatonic state.

"Are you alright, Vitya?" I asked him.

"I... I... cannot take it any longer," he muttered under his breath.

"What?"

"All of that... My dead mum, cats, dogs, no internet, useless phones, the house that is seemingly ours, and yet not quite; the police spelled with an 's'... This unending nightmare!"

"I agree, it is extremely annoying, but what can we do? Fly to Majorca and join the Ks? I am sure you wouldn't mind having another good snog with Katherine."

"Just like you with Viktor. No, this is not what I am thinking."

Like Elvira a short time ago, my husband jumped off the sofa with unexpected prowess.

"I have an idea. We've got the car back at last. Why don't we try and recreate the crash now, straightaway, by ourselves, without waiting for police supervision? You never know, we may succeed at the first go."

"Vitya, don't be silly. This is too risky. What if we miscalculate and end up getting killed or badly injured?"

"We will be careful, Catia. Very careful. And even if I get killed, I frankly do not care. It is better to be dead than to live in this horrible universe!"

"What if just one of us gets killed? I myself do not fancy dying just yet. What if we both become invalids?"

"I told you – we'll take precautions. But we must try it now. There is no choice. Unless you are dying to try my dead mum's cutlets of course."

The thought of Elvira's cooking, enhanced by the continuing barking and hissing of the fighting pets from the garden, where the live fluffy ball had ended up by then, helped me to take the decision.

"OK, Vitya. I will count on you. But please, please, please, let's proceed with caution!"

At this point, the reader may start wondering what had happened to Professor Spiegeltent and Superintendent Burgess since they parted company with the Ks and the Cs.

Having put the Ks on the day's last flight from Stansted to Palma and having made sure they had gone through customs, Professor Spiegeltent drove home, where he quickly packed his suitcase and said to his wife that he had to be off on an urgent research assignment. He then drove to another nearby airport, Lowton, from where, as he knew, a later Colinair flight to Palma was due to depart. To his delight, there were still several seats available, and soon the Professor was airborne. The plane landed in Palma at 1.30 am local time next morning. Even after the funds allocated to the Ks, there was still enough left in his research budget to cover a week-long car hire at the airport. Spiegeltent then drove to Port de Polenca, and by 2.30 am, only an hour behind the Ks, he was in his hotel on the Promenade, next to the one where the couple were put up for the night. He woke up at half past five in the morning, checked out, got into his hired car and discreetly followed the coach carrying Viktor and Katherine, all the way to Palma. The Ks of course never looked back at the sleek black Volkswagen, but even if they did, they wouldn't have been able to recognise its driver sporting large thick sunglasses behind the wheel.

Spiegeltent was having the time of his life. At last he was again part of an important, possibly ground-breaking and prize-winning, research effort – a welcome change from teaching maths to a bunch of lazy and ignorant youngsters.

In Palma, he did his best to follow the couple everywhere they went to make sure they kept doing the right thing. So far, he was pleased with the Ks who seemed to be taking their mission very seriously. When Katherine and Viktor temporarily split up to do their own thing each, Spiegeltent allowed himself a short break and had a quick snooze on a park bench before heading towards the restaurant where he knew they would meet up for lunch. From the window table of a small coffee shop opposite the restaurant, he had a good view of the *al fresco* terrace where the couple were sitting. Spiegeltent knew that his help would be needed soon.

As for Superintendent Burgess, his task was both easier and harder than his friend's. Easier – because he did not have to fly anywhere, not yet, but simply sat inside an unmarked police car, parked in the shadow of a tree across the road from the dead couple's cottage – on the same spot where the Petroffs' Volvo was parked the other day when the Ks thought they had been burgled. Harder – because he was unable to allow himself even a short rest, he just kept watching the brightly lit-up windows of the cottage, behind which the Cs and Elvira were arguing, and waiting for further developments which, he knew, could occur any moment.

Chapter Fifteen

A Reluctant Oyster

Professor Spiegeltent could see Viktor going inside the restaurant and reaching for his phone as he walked. There was only one person in the universe Viktor had the correct number for: himself.

In less than ten seconds, the Professor's phone began vibrating.

"Professor? Good afternoon. It's me, Viktor Petroff."

"So I guessed," Spiegeltent replied. "Is everything ok?"

"I wouldn't be calling you if it were, Professor. We… My wife and I are in a restaurant in Palma, the same restaurant where Katherine got food poisoning on our previous visit. So far, we've been trying to repeat all our movements to the letter, but now we feel a bit stuck."

"What's the problem?"

"We are about to order our food. But how can we make sure there will be a bad prawn or, say, scallop, in our meal? We cannot specifically request one, can we?"

"Hmm… I see… It may be difficult indeed," the Professor was frantically thinking of a solution. Suddenly he had an idea.

"Are you sitting inside the restaurant, or outside in an open terrace, if any?" The Professor already knew the answer, but had to ask this question so as not to give away his own whereabouts.

"Outside of course. It's scorching hot here, about 500 degrees Fahrengrade, I would say."

Spiegeltent had no idea what 'Fahrengrade' meant, but assumed it was hot enough for what he was about to suggest.

"Great! Why don't you order fresh oysters, but don't eat them straight away. Put the dish under direct sunlight and wait for about twenty minutes. Twenty-five to be on the safe side."

"What are we supposed to wait for?" Viktor sounded puzzled. And somewhat nettled too.

"Oysters are extremely sensitive to heat and don't stay fresh for very long even in a fridge. That is why they should ideally be consumed within a couple of hours after being caught. Any qualified chef would tell you that it takes twenty minutes of direct hot sunlight to turn a fresh oyster into a bad one. Guaranteed!"

"I see!" exclaimed Viktor. "You are a genius, Professor! But what are we going to do while we wait? We are also very hungry."

"Order a soup. Or a salad. Or anything… and ask the waiter to bring all of those together with the oysters."

"Will do, Professor. Will do. Thank you ever so much. My next challenge is to persuade Katherine to go through it again… Easier said than done… Does it have to be her who gets poisoned? Or can I do it for a change perhaps?"

"Viktor, you have already answered your question. To stand any chance of success, we have to keep the 'change' element to an absolute minimum. To zero ideally. Your altruism is commendable, and I am sure your wife will appreciate it properly after she recovers from her ordeal."

"What if she dies of food poisoning?"

"Did she last time? She won't on this occasion either. Just make sure you take her to hospital and feed her all the right medicines, as before. And hurry up: your wife's notes tell me that she was already feeling unwell this time a week ago."

"Thank you, Professor. I will do exactly as you say!"

In less than a minute, Spiegeltent saw Viktor emerge from inside the restaurant. He hurried back to his table and immediately beckoned the waiter. Spiegeltent stood up, and, having put some euro coins on the table, left the coffee shop. He knew that for the next half-hour or so the couple were going to stay put. Watching Katherine throw up was not a spectacle to look forward to…

"So, how are you feeling, darling?" Viktor asked Katherine forty minutes later, about ten minutes after she duly, with her eyes tightly shut, swallowed a couple of large juicy '*ostras*', trying not to smell them and washing them down with a large glass of ice-cold white Rioja.

"Don't you darling me, Vitya. Not now. I am starting to feel a bit queasy, with some discomfort in my tummy. Shall we pay the bill and go?"

"Not yet, Katia, not yet. You may not remember, but your first attack of sickness happened right here, in the restaurant."

"I do hope this is going to work, Vitya. Whatever universe we are in, I swear I am not going through this ag…"

She never finished the sentence. A projectile of vomit burst out of her mouth. Some of it landed on the starchy while tablecloth and the rest – on her husband's T-shirt.

"Here it comes!" mumbled Viktor wrinkling his nose. "Well done, darling. Give us another one, will you?"

Katherine didn't need to be asked twice. From the corner of her eye, she could see patrons at the neighbouring tables jump off their chairs and run away in disgust. A blurred silhouette of the waiter was towering above her repeating worriedly: "*Estas bien, signora? Estas bien?*"

On their tiptoes, trying not to alert Elvira, frantically cooking her famous *katleti* in the kitchen, Catherine and Victor sneaked out of the front door into the driveway where their Volvo was parked. It was dark and already very late, so the Cs managed to leave the cottage and get into their car unnoticed by anyone. How about our vigilant Superintendent Burgess, you may ask? Well, after such a busy eventful day, is it any wonder that he nodded off behind the wheel of the unmarked police (or rather **'polise'**) car, parked under a tree across the road, and did not see the couple either.

Victor was very careful to start the car as gently as he could, without much noise – and off they drove towards the motorway.

"How soon should I try and attempt the crash?" he asked his wife when they left the town and drove into the pitch-dark countryside.

"The crash happened about twenty minutes after we left the airport, so why don't we drive around for a short while before going for it?" Catherine replied from the front passenger seat. "And please promise me again you will be careful," she added.

"Don't worry, Cat, I will be."

For twenty minutes or so, they roamed about the dark and empty Z1 motorway.

"It's good there are no other cars around," Catherine commented. "I do not really want to have some innocent people involved in our car accident, like last time."

"Well, darling, they were not so innocent, those guys: underage and uninsured. Besides, if there are no other cars or people around, who is going to help us out of our crashed car and alert the police?"

"Vitya, you promised!" snapped up Catherine. "We should be able to get out of the car and alert the police ourselves! And, hopefully, this time it will be 'police' with a 'c', not **'polise'** with an 's'!"

Silence followed.

"Are you ready, Cat? I am about to try now," Victor declared finally without taking his eyes off the motorway. "That patch of forest looks promising."

Catherine squinted at the unlit road and was able to discern some dark tree shapes in the distance. The shapes were approaching quickly. Or rather the Cs were dashing towards them at seventy-five miles per hour.

"God help us!" she whispered.

"And Spiegeltent help us too," Victor mumbled and turned the wheel to the left sharply.

A loud bang followed as the Petrovs' Volvo hit a tree trunk. That was the only thing Catherine was acutely aware of initially. She was sprayed with fragments of broken glass, some of which scratched her face rather painfully. It was only then that she felt the impact of the crash as her body was thrown forward towards the windscreen, now covered with an inflated airbag, and – halted by the fastened seat belt – pulled back into the seat violently. She felt a sharp pain in her ribs, which hadn't quite healed after the previous accident.

Victor's head was resting on the steering wheel, his forehead pressing on the horn. He was fully conscious, just shocked and dazed momentarily.

From the corner of her eye, Catherine could see a couple of cars on the motorway – where had they come from? – stopping, their lights blinking. In no time, the characteristic wailing of police sirens could be heard.

With an effort, Victor lifted his head off the wheel.

"Are you ok, Catia?"

Catherine was motionless – strapped to her seat, with her eyes wide open. For a minute or so, she didn't respond. Through the haze that enveloped her vision, she could see a small patch of the motorway, now crowded with cars, half of which were police vehicles.

"Yes, Vitya, I am ok," she said at last, feeling the characteristic salty taste of blood in her mouth. "I am ok, but we have failed."

Victor looked up. Through the yawning gap in the Volvo's front, where the windscreen used to be only moments ago, he saw some uniformed men jump out of stationary cars and run towards the crash spot. "**Polise**" was written in big letters on the sides of the cars, straight underneath the blinking blue lights on their roofs.

In front of the running policemen, as Victor was able to register before fainting briefly, was Peter Burgess in his easily identifiable Superintendent's uniform with snow-white lapels.

Chapter Sixteen

Incidental Accidents

"What… what do we do now?" Viktor muttered when Katherine, pale and shivering, returned to the terrace, having vomited her guts out, or so she felt, in the restaurant toilet. Despite expecting it, the shock of what happened was such that he completely forgot the order of actions they had to stick to.

"Hospital…" his wife whispered semi-audibly.

Yes, of course. So scared were the Petroffs by the sudden sickness attack a week earlier that they took a taxi to the AED – or *'Urgencias'* in Spanish – department of Son Espases – Majorca's main state-run hospital. That proved fairly useless, for the only thing the doctors could do was to give Katherine a handful of stomach-fixing pills. Now they had to go there again, there was no option.

The same woman as ten days before was at the AED's reception desk. She looked at the Petroffs with astonishment.

"*De nuevo?* (Again?)" she scowled and pointed them to the waiting area.

Like most Brits, Katherine and Viktor did not tend to associate the normally cheerful, talkative and robust Balearians with disease. They had read books about some Greek and other islands famous for their healthy diets and the islanders' longevity and therefore could be forgiven for assuming that all Greeks, Italians or, say, Majorcans were generally healthy. Seeing them in the *'Urgencias'* department of Son Espases hospital being sick – and some of them appeared very poorly indeed – ruined the stereotype.

The doctor who saw Katherine was not the one that had attended to her previously, but there was nothing the Petroffs could do about it: they couldn't possibly demand that Katherine be seen by the same doctor as a week earlier, and could only hope that the change was not going to affect the final result of their quest.

Just as before, the doctor examined Katherine, listened to her heart through a stethoscope, measured her blood pressure and, having called Viktor in, announced what they already knew: that she had severe food poisoning and needed complete rest.

"But we are supposed to be flying back to the UK this afternoon," Viktor objected meekly.

"Out of the question!" the doctor, who, unlike the receptionist, spoke good English, said firmly. "Your wife needs to rest for at least a couple of days. So if I were you, I would cancel or change your flights *con rapidez* and find a nice hotel where she can recuperate."

There was no need for Katherine and Viktor to look for a 'nice hotel'. They knew only too well which hotel they had to stay at, and not just the hotel but the room too.

Plenty of taxis, with blue lights above the roofs, were waiting outside the hospital's main entrance.

'Blu Cab Company' was written on their doors.

"Why... why... do they have blue lights on, not green?" Katherine – pale and shivering – asked her husband semi-audibly.

"No idea," replied Viktor. "Let's hope that blue lights in this universe mean that the cabs are free for hire. I am more puzzled by the way 'blue' is spelled in what is obviously their local version of English – without an 'e' in the end..."

Having commandeered the first 'blu' cab in the row, they climbed in. "*BonSol hotel, por favore,*" Viktor said to the driver who nodded and switched on the ignition. As the taxi was leaving the vast Son Espases hospital yard, Professor Spiegeltent ran out of the hospital building, jumped into the next 'blu' cab in the queue and asked the driver to follow the Ks. He knew where the couple were going, and just wanted to make sure they did not deviate from their route of ten days ago.

Hotel BonSol in Iletas was less than half an hour's drive from the hospital along the motorway, but, just like on the previous occasion, Viktor told the driver to take them via central Palma, where he popped out to pick up their suitcases from the obliging owner of 'San Joan de S'Aigo' café. When out of the city, they had to pull over to allow Katherine to throw up in the bushes near the curb. On the way, Viktor also managed to use his mobile phone to cancel their flights. "We won't get the full cost back, just sixty percent, due to a late cancellation," he announced grimly to his wife, who couldn't care less and said so.

It was all going largely to plan, except for several small deviations.

BonSol's vast and permanently semi-dark – to beat the heat – lobby was empty, apart from Pablo, an elderly concierge nodding behind his desk, and Olga, the receptionist, who was always polite and had been extremely helpful to the Petroffs during their previous stay.

"I cannot to believe my eyes!" she exclaimed, with a strong Spanish accent, on seeing the couple. "Viktor! Katherina! How nicely to see you! I did not know you was coming to us again!"

"*Hola*, Olga," smiled Viktor. "Yes, we are back, and – just like last time – we were not able to pre-book, sorry…"

"*No te preocupes*! Don't worry! We are not foolish, and can find you a nice *habitacion*!"

She meant the hotel was not full, of course.

"*Gracias*, Olga," said Viktor. "The problem is that Katherine is not well again. She very much liked room 25, where we stayed last time. She says that the room itself, the sea views and all the rest, had actually helped her recover."

He turned to his wife, who – weak as she was – was nodding enthusiastically.

"We would be so happy if you could accommodate us in our old room 25, if possible," Viktor continued.

"Un momento!" Olga turned her head to the computer screen in front of her, typed something quickly without looking down at the keyboard – and frowned.

"Les ruego me perdonen, excuse me, but room 25 is occupied… A very nice couple *ruso…* But I can give to you another nice *habitacion –* in the building across the road. It is very good and more close to the sea."

Viktor was in shock.

"Olga, I don't know how to explain this to you, but it is essential for us to stay in that particular room – 25 – and no other!"

"Yes… please, Olga…" Katherine whispered from behind her husband's back.

"But this not possible!" Like many Majorcans, Olga could easily fluctuate between a most benign disposition and anger. "I was telling to you that *Senor y Senora* Kuchkin are living there. They booked in advance and are not leaving soon. You talk to them if they want to change…"

"Could YOU talk to them please?"

"Nunca! Never!" shouted Olga as she stormed out from her behind-the-counter office and out of the building into the lush subtropical garden, from where the crickets' early-evening chorus could already be heard.

The Petroffs' whole mission was suddenly under threat.

"What are we going to do now?" Viktor asked his wife rhetorically.

"We are… going… to try and talk to the Kuchkins," Katherine murmured – green-faced – and dashed towards the nearest bathroom.

All three of them: Catherine, Victor and Superintendent Burgess – were sitting on a neatly-made bed in a cubicle behind a paper screen inside the Accident and Emergency department of Camford General Hospital, where they had been driven by paramedics after their unfortunate and botched – in more than one sense – car accident.

Victor looked shocked and very pale, but otherwise unharmed, whereas Catherine had a deep scratch in the middle of her forehead now covered with white plaster.

"So, why did you let me down? Why didn't you listen to what Professor Spiegeltent had to say?" Superintendent Burgess, sitting on the sharp edge of the hospital bed which made him feel fidgety and unsettled, asked the Cs.

"And what exactly did he say? I cannot recall now," Victor responded after a pause.

"He said that car crash imitations, if any, must be conducted under strict police supervision and that you should try at least ten times to see if any of them works."

"Well, I think we kind of got fed up with the situation and decided that we didn't want to wait any longer," shrugged Victor.

"Yes, and nearly killed yourselves as a result!" Burgess jumped up and started pacing up and down the cubicle. "You guys are lucky to be alive and uninjured, do you realise that? When you are dead, it doesn't matter which universe you are in!"

"You may be wrong on that point, Mr Burgess," Victor objected timidly. "By the laws of quantum mechanics, we may be dead in one dimension and perfectly alive and fine in another. Have you heard of Schrodinger's cat, by any chance?"

"I studied the basics of physics at school, together with Professor Spiegeltent, by the way, and know only too well that Schrodinger's cat, who is simultaneously dead and alive, is not a certainty but simply a thought experiment, whereas your so-called experiment was entirely thoughtless. And selfish too. Did you think what effect your death was going to have on other people, like, say, myself, officially responsible for your well-being? Rest assured that from now on, I won't let you out of my sight for a single moment. Not until we complete all ten car-accident re-enactments!"

At this point, the Superintendent's protracted monologue was interrupted by Catherine.

"I am not doing any more re-enactments," she said calmly. "For me, enough is enough".

"What do you mean, Catia?" shouted Victor. "Don't you want us to go back home?"

"I don't want to die. Not yet. I want us to have children before it is too late and to grow old happily. Either here or there… I don't care."

"But next time we'll do it under police supervision, so we'll be safe," Victor insisted.

"You do it alone, if you wish, Vitya. I won't be taking part. And that is my last word."

Victor knew his wife only too well to keep arguing further.

An awkward silence followed, broken only by the usual hospital sounds – bleeps of medical gadgets, muffled moans of patients. Superintendent Burgess stood up and paced the cubicle nervously.

It was Catherine who finally spoke.

"Call me dumb, but I find it hard to understand why we can't join the Ks in Majorca," she said. "After all, apart from the damned car crash, we all had gone through roughly the same stuff: unexpected delay with returning home, air turbulence during the flight… Who knows at which point we stumbled out of our normal world?"

"But Catia, don't you see that it is much easier to re-enact food poisoning than a jellyfish sting? Since we are at least in some control of our stomachs, we could deliberately ingest something not fresh or outright rotten, as I am sure your lovely double is going to do, but how on earth could we find an agreeable jellyfish and persuade it to sting my hand?"

"I don't see a big problem here, Vitya," his wife replied. "There are normally hundreds of jellyfish off any Majorcan beach this time of the year. I know this might be unpleasant and even painful for you, but still much better than dying in a car crash, police-controlled or not."

It was now Burgess's turn to speak out. He was secretly pleased by the turn the conversation was taking. Organising and supervising car accidents was not something he was looking forward to as a policeman, even if his old friend had asked him to do so.

"I think Catherine may be right," he said at last. "Car crashes, no matter how well-organised and executed, always carry a huge element of risk. Of course, I am not as familiar with the probability theory as my professor friend, but I trust Catherine is also right in saying that your unintended... er... trespassing – let's use a police term here – into an alternative universe might have occurred earlier: during the flight back home, or even before it while you were still in Majorca. There's of course no point in staging further car accidents, if Catherine is not taking part in them, and we cannot – and should not – expect her to do so against her will."

He looked at his watch.

"What time is it in Majorca now? They are one hour ahead of us, so it must be quite late. But I will try to call Daniel, I mean Professor Spiegeltent, straight away and ask for his advice. If he is not yet asleep of course... Give me an hour – and don't try to escape from the hospital please!"

"What would be the point in us escaping when we have nowhere to go to?" sighed Victor.

The Petrovs did not have a chance to talk to each other properly. Straight after Burgess's hasty departure a nurse came in to measure their blood pressure and do other routine tests. The moment she left the cubicle, the policeman barged back in.

"I've managed to get hold of Dan... Professor Spiegeltent," he puffed out. "In principle, he agreed with Catherine's suggestion and said that his department's modest research funds could probably cover your trip to Majorca too. As well as mine, for he wants me to accompany you there. But again, he asked me to stress that – as in the case of the Ks – there are no guarantees whatsoever of a successful outcome. So if you are still willing to go ahead with this endeavour, or shall we call it a scientific experiment, we could all take the first morning flight to Palma. Unless of course the medics want to keep you under observation here for any longer..."

"No, they've just given us the all clear," Victor lied.

"Great. Hope they won't throw you out until the morning which should give you enough time to rest after your self-imposed ordeal. And also – just as your… er… friends, the Ks, did earlier – to recall, write down and time your exact movements and actions during your previous stay in Majorca. Meanwhile, I am going to leave you to arrange the flights, tidy up a couple of urgent cases at the office and get packed myself."

"How about our travel bags? I need my make-up and a change of clothes," Catherine remarked.

"No worries. I am going to instruct a constable to pick up your luggage from the cottage and drop it at the airport tomorrow morning."

"God, he is like a human tempest," commented Catherine after Burgess had dashed out of the room, and the paper screen around the bed on which the Cs were sitting was still stirring from the wind created by the policeman's speedy departure.

"Don't tell me you started fancying him, Catia. From what I know, men in uniform have never been your type," Victor said.

"Unlike your wife's doubles for yourself," Catherine retorted.

"I wouldn't go there, if I were you," Victor wagged his finger at her, and – for the first time since the accident – they both smiled.

It was only when they were already airborne the next morning that Superintendent Burgess, sitting in front of the Petrovs, turned to them and said: "Forgot to tell you yesterday, but Professor Spiegeltent insists that while in Majorca you must have no contact whatsoever with your… er… opposite numbers, who have to stick to their own schedule and itinerary, even if you happen to be in close proximity to each other. According to his calculations, failure to do so may seriously jeopardise the success of the mission – both yours and theirs – and lead to some truly unpredictable consequences."

He turned away from the Cs and was unable to see the expression of disappointment, even misery, on their faces. For a fleeting moment, both Catherine and Victor came to regret their decision to fly to Majorca. But it was too late to change course. One couldn't just go up to the captain and say: "Could you please stop the plane, for I want to get off?"

Their flight to Palma was smooth and turbulence-free.

Chapter Seventeen

Accidental Incidents

To get to room 25, situated in a different wing of the hotel, Viktor and Katherine had to first walk through the vast and ornate ground-floor lobby, generously decorated with paintings, sculptures, statues of Buddhas – both jolly Chinese ones, smiling, hedonistic and with large round bellies, and Indian, immersed in meditation – and other artefacts brought from their travels by the members of the agreeable and highly cultured English-Spanish family of the hotel owners. In the corner of the lobby, there was a small, yet cosy and alluring, exchange library, where the guests could leave the books they had finished reading and borrow the unread ones instead.

They then had to walk the length of a long, dimly lit and pleasantly cool underground corridor, connecting two hotel wings. In the middle of the candle-lit passage, in a small cave, carved in the rock, was a miniature chapel.

At the end of the corridor was a lift which took the Petroffs to the second floor. They soon stood in front of room 25, which had a 'Do Not Disturb' sign stuck to the door handle, unsure how to proceed.

"They are probably out," whispered Viktor. "Shall we come back later?"

"They may actually be in – asleep, making love, or just watching telly," objected Katherine. "Why don't you knock to make sure? Remember: we don't have a lot of time?"

Viktor sighed and knocked on the door gently.

Silence.

"What did I tell you, Katia? They are not…"

Before Viktor could finish the sentence the door swung open, narrowly missing his head. A hairy ruddy-faced man, wearing nothing under the white dressing gown with 'BonSol' embroidered above the breast pocket, was staring at the couple with badly concealed menace.

"Can't you read?" he asked in heavily accented English pointing at the sign.

"We are so sorry, Mr Kuchkin," Viktor mumbled, "but my wife is unwell, and we have to speak with you urgently."

"Your wife could be dead for all I know, but that still wouldn't give you the right to knock on the door with a 'Do Not Disturb' sign on it!"

The man tried to shut the door in Viktor's face, just like Victor had several days earlier, and again – just like then, when he was trying to gain entrance to the cottage which he had thought was his and Katherine's – he put his foot through the door.

"Listen, we've got a proposition," he insisted. "And if you are interested, there may be something for you in it too."

Kuchkin stopped pushing. He stared first at Viktor, then at Katherine, with her head down, hiding behind her husband's back, and must have decided that they did not look like the Russian mafia debt collectors.

Instead of inviting the couple in, he stepped – bare-foot – into the corridor and closed the door of the room behind him.

"What proposition? Be quick!"

Viktor burst into a long diatribe explaining how precious room 25 was to them. It was, allegedly, the room where they stayed during their honeymoon exactly fifteen years ago, and it was important for them, particularly for his wife, who was not feeling well, to stay in that very room now, when they had come to Majorca to celebrate their wedding anniversary. He was inventing the story while he was telling it.

"In view of all that and to compensate you for the inconvenience, we will be happy to offer you a hundred euros in cash for moving to another room, and if that room happens to be more expensive than room 25, we will of course pay off the difference too."

Viktor finished his monologue and looked at Mr Kuchkin pleadingly. The latter – visibly taken aback by such an unusual request – stared back at him saying nothing. It was so quiet in the hotel corridor that one could probably hear a fly sneeze; only Katherine's subdued hiccups could be heard every now and then.

All of sudden, Kuchkin burst out laughing in Victor's face.

"Ha-ha-ha! *Kak smeshno*! How funny! Ha-ha-ha!"

The Petroffs went numb.

"Ha-ha-ha!" Kuchkin opened the door to the room slightly and shouted into the gap: "Masha! Masha! *Idi siuda*! Come here fast!"

A fat middle-aged woman in exactly the same white dressing gown as her husband's, emerged from the room. She must have been snoozing and was blinking her little red eyes sleepily.

"*Chto takoye*? What's up, Mishen'ka?"

"Masha, *posmotri na etikh nenormal'nikh*! Look at these two mad people here! They want us to move out of our room for a hundred euros! Can you believe it?"

It was now Katherine's turn to repeat for Mrs Kuchkina – between bouts of hiccups – the cock-and-bull story about their alleged wedding anniversary.

Mrs Kuchkina, however, appeared more sensitive than her husband.

"You know, Misha," she said, having heard Katherine out, "*Ya ikh ponimayu...* I actually sympathise with them. Remember our honeymoon in that rather dodgy hotel in Leningrad? I think we – as warm and kind people – should help them."

"Thank you, thank you ever so much..." Viktor began as Mrs Kuchkina went on without listening to him.

"Of course, we won't move anywhere tonight, so they will have to wait until tomorrow afternoon, or better – until the day after tomorrow... And, of course, I won't take a single step out of this lovely room for some miserable hundred euros. But for three thousand I might!"

Viktor felt as if he was suddenly splashed with ice-cold water.

"But… but… we do not have that kind of money," he muttered. "Besides, we really must move into your room now, by tomorrow morning at the latest."

"Tomorrow morning? *Zavtra utrom?* You want tomorrow morning?" roared Mr Kuchkin. "Yes, we can do tomorrow morning, why not? But that will cost you five thousand euros and not a single euro cent less! In fact, for five grand we'll be out of here in a jiffy any time of night or day, won't we Mashen'ka? Think about it!"

"But please… please… be merciful… Don't do this to us…" Katherine pleaded. "You know, my husband has Russian roots, like you do. Wouldn't you be willing to help your compatriot out?"

That was a mistake.

"*Russkiy?* Russian?" yelled Mr Kuchkin. "You mean he is an emigrant? A traitor? Probably even a dissident? My wife already told you that we are good and merciful people, and that was why we agreed to help you for five thousand euros. And if you don't want me to raise the fee to ten thousand, stop talking about your husband being Russian. We don't like traitors! Let's go, Masha!"

The moment the door slammed shut behind the Kuchkins, Katherine and Viktor could hear them giggling inside the room. They must have been extremely pleased with themselves.

"I hate these New Russians, these fat money bags! The oligarchs! They are robbing my poor motherland!" exploded Viktor. "They bring shame and disgrace to the whole nation!"

"Come off it, Vitya. They are your former compatriots, after all. Just a bit luckier than most perhaps. We'd better think of where we could get the money from. Should I perhaps become an escort girl for the night?"

"Not with your food poisoning, darling, for who would want a constantly vomiting escort, even if a pretty one?"

"Which reminds me…" Katherine muttered and ran away.

She returned in five minutes – grey in the face but looking relieved.

"I've been thinking about it, Katia," Viktor said. "There's no other option but to call the Professor again. He may be able to suggest something."

He took out his mobile and typed in Spiegeltent's number.

From Professor Spiegeltent's Dossier:

The first day in Majorca, where I was meant to covertly provide back-up and counselling (if needed) for the Petroffs, proved very busy and therefore successful (if I may say so), if not for the couple themselves, then definitely for yours truly. By that I mean that my research was progressing smoothly, without a hitch, and Viktor Petroff made me feel useful (and hence less doubtful about whether this highly unusual – if not to say weird – project offered valid reasons for blowing ninety percent of my department's annual research budget on it).

My brief, as agreed with my old friend and colleague Superintendent Peter Burgess, was to follow the couple wherever they went in Majorca without making my presence obvious. The latter precaution was dictated solely by the Calculus of Probabilities, which, in the words of James Clerk Maxwell, represented the only true logic for this world, and for all other existing worlds (or so I want to hope). In plain words (and, as I wrote already, those are the words I did and will try to stick to while writing this dossier), anything or anyone that was not part of the scenario, which led the Petroffs to inadvertently cross into an alternative universe, should be kept out of the experiment aimed at recreating that same scenario. Here I can only add that the fundamental problem of scientific progress is that of learning from past experience. Knowledge obtained in this way is partly merely description of what we have already observed, but partly consists of making inferences from past experience to predict future experience.

I'd better stop this short excursion to the realms of logic and probability before any lay reader of this dossier, who is not a mathematician by education, pushes it aside...

I managed to successfully follow the Petroffs all the way from Port de Pollenca to Palma, and was pleased to observe them showing initiative and considerable ingenuity in trying to procure for themselves the same seats on the coach in which they travelled previously, and eventually succeeding. They also tried to stick strictly to their initial itinerary when in Palma, with no significant deviations that could even further reduce the already infinitesimal probability of their return home.

The first hitch appeared when food poisoning had to be induced in poor Katherine, whom I had come to like a lot in those few hours we had been working together for her intelligence, quick wit and her pragmatic no-nonsense attitude to life's problems (I have to add here that I came to like her 'opposite number' – I don't like the word 'double' – Catherine, too, which, due to their incredible likeness, for they were basically one and the same person, should not be surprising). Having heroically agreed to sacrifice her immediate health for the sake of the experiment, Katherine was at a loss as to how exactly the poisoning could be executed. And so was Viktor, her husband, who decided to call me from a seafood restaurant on my mobile number which, for the reasons explained above, I had advised him to use only in cases of extreme emergency. Well, that was definitely one of them.

The couple's problem was how to quickly turn fresh and healthy seafood into something bad and rotten. Luckily, I knew the answer from a professional chef friend of mine, who once told me in confidence never to order fresh oysters in restaurants, if I wanted to avoid food poisoning. "Oysters are the most sensitive, the most perishable products you can imagine," he said. "Leave a perfect freshly caught oyster under direct sunlight for just twenty minutes – and I can guarantee it will go rotten!"

So, I advised him accordingly, and – from my unsophisticated shelter in a café across the road from the seafood restaurant they were in – was soon able to make sure that it all worked beautifully for our project, if not immediately for poor Katherine, who soon became a kind of a vomiting human volcano, but – again – was taking it all with remarkable stoicism. I could only hope they hadn't overdone it and she was in for a fast recovery.

I followed the Ks to Son Espases Hospital, where, I was sure, it would take them at least two or three hours to subject Katherine to all the necessary tests and procedures (not including the inevitable waiting time in all A&E departments of the world), and thought that would give me ample time to explore the interiors of BonSol Hotel for the existence of an alternative universe portal, before the Petroffs came to stay there, as I very much hoped they would.

Having made sure the Petroffs were inside the hospital, I drove to Iletas and found the hotel easily. I introduced myself at the reception as a potential BonSol guest who wanted to take a good look around before booking a room and was given an all-clear to wander wherever I wanted. They even gave me a plastic electronic pass for the multiple in-house lifts. I was told the hotel had a number of floors and layers, all built into a large rock, which used to serve as a natural fortress to shelter the locals from the aggressive Moors who would attack the town from the sea.

I started with the impressively stocked exchange library in the corner of the extremely ornate and richly decorated, yet still surprisingly cosy, first-floor lobby. The shelves were sagging under the books in many different languages, and I was pleased, albeit not particularly surprised, to find a beautifully preserved copy of a 'Guide to Majorca', published in the Republic of Tavrida in year 4891. No wonder the book was not in big demand and looked almost like new.

I was now a hundred percent certain that the mysterious Man from Tavrida did exist and did stay at this very hotel. The only question that remained was how he had actually got there.

For the next two hours, I used a portable infra-red quantum-particle scanner, developed to my specifications by the colleagues from the engineering department of our university shortly after I heard the story of the Man from Tavrida twenty-five odd years ago and unused since then. The gadget resembles a fountain pen with a laser light at the top. With its help, I very thoroughly explored all the hotel's numerous nooks and crannies, its secret doors under the stairs leading to well-hidden closets and storage rooms, its underground tunnels, which – depending on the situation – used to serve as hiding places for the locals, escaping from the invading Moors, or as passages for all kinds of smugglers.

In short, it was an ideal place for a portal to a different dimension, except for the fact that I failed to find one. By the end of my search, I was pretty sure that it simply did not exist anywhere on or near the hotel grounds. That meant the Man from Tavrida as well as the Ks had got here by some other means, and the fact that they found themselves staying in the same hotel twenty years apart was nothing but another coincidence.

Any coincidence can of course be explained as pure chance, whereas to others the probability laws can be applied. Gustav Carl Elder, the famous psychologist and philosopher, believed that it was the so-called synchronicity, which he himself defined as a causal connecting principle, that was behind the large number of seemingly coincidental occurrences, which he branded 'meaningful coincidences'. Yet I was (and still am) inclined to regard the fact that the Ks and the Man from Tavrida stayed at the same hotel as the former, i.e. pure chance, or, using Elder's terminology, a totally 'meaningless' coincidence, rather than synchronicity, for there was no causal connection whatsoever between those two happenings. And the best proof of that was the second couple, the Cs, who had actually managed to avoid BonSol altogether, and stayed at another hotel in Palma. I was surprised and rather annoyed that neither I nor Peter Burgess had thought about this earlier. Moreover that both of us must have been well aware of the widely reported recent scientific breakthrough whereby a group of astronomers from Darhum University found a strange area in the sky that could be reflecting the consequence of a collision between two different universes – the first ever practical evidence of the theory of the multiverse: that there are billions of other universes, some of them just like our own, lurking outside the one that we can see. Again, they found it in the SKY, straight above our heads!

Suddenly, I realised very clearly that the only thing shared by both couples and the Man from Tavrida was... the flight from Majorca to the UK, so if the trespassing into the alterative world did occur in each of the three cases, it could have only happened in the air somewhere between Majorca and the UK. That in turn meant that the portal, if any, could only be located in the skies, and therefore any further searches in BonSol or anywhere else were bound to prove futile. On the other hand, the latter scenario, multiplied by the probability laws, enhanced the necessity for both couples (or both versions of one and the same couple, as some would prefer to regard the Ks and the Cs) to stick to all their initial movements to the letter, if they wanted to stand any chance whatsoever of crossing over back to their respective worlds.

I was in a hurry to share my findings with Peter, but my friend was ahead of me and called first.

I was not particularly surprised by the Cs' decision to fly to Majorca. Each of the four (or each of the two) 'actors' in this unusual situation was physiologically justified in feeling physical attraction to his or her spouse's near-double – a slightly modified and hence fairly irresistible variation of his/her attraction to the real-life husband/wife. The problem with that was the same as I tried to describe earlier while explaining to the Ks why I could not be with them at all times: not to undermine the Calculus of Probabilities, according to which anything or anyone that was **not** part of the initial scenario was to be kept out of the experiment aimed at recreating it. That meant that under no circumstances should the Cs and the Ks be allowed to have any contact with each other – physical, visual or even audio. In general, however, I agreed that it made some sense to bring the Cs here too, only perhaps there was no need for them to travel to Pollenca. They could pick up their movements and begin recreating them starting with the jellyfish sting accident on a beach.

"I think, my friend, that you should come over here too," I said to Peter. "To clandestinely keep your vigilant policeman's eye on the Petrovs, assist them in emergencies, if any, and keep them apart from the Ks."

"But, Daniel, I am up to my ears in running the station which will slide into chaos if I were to go away," Peter tried to object.

"It won't, for you will only be away for several days," I said. "Besides, you can do with a bit of a break yourself, or so I think."

He finally agreed and asked me if I had found anything of interest in BonSol.

"That must have been a coincidence. I scanned the hotel inside out with my infra-red equipment; no portal. The transgression must have happened during the flight," I explained.

"But how about the Tavrida-printed World Atlas, which I found in the K's suitcase?"

"They must have borrowed it from the hotel's exchange library: it didn't belong to them."

We finished the conversation by agreeing a meeting place in Palma for the day after next when we could start organising separate flights back to the UK for each couple.

It all sounded reassuring, and little did I know then that it was my very last conversation with my friend Peter Burgess.

Chapter Eighteen

Roulette Rules

Having finished speaking with Superintendent Burgess, Professor Spiegeltent packed up his infra-red scanner and headed for the BonSol's main bar next to the reception to wait for the Ks' arrival. He ordered a large vodka martini and sat in the bar's far corner, with a good view of the lobby, to make sure he could see everyone approaching the reception without being easily spotted himself.

He didn't have to wait for very long. The couple soon entered the lobby, Viktor holding his wife's hand. Even from the distance of several dozen metres, Spiegeltent could not help noticing how weak and pale Katherine looked.

They had a brief, yet rather heated, verbal exchange with the receptionist. Spiegeltent could not hear what the parties were saying but could guess that room 25, where he knew the Petroffs had stayed last time, must have been the apple of discord.

"I bet the room is occupied by someone else," he thought. That could mean only one thing: Viktor was bound to call him for advice again soon.

And he was right: his phone rang persistently in less than half an hour.

Viktor's voice in the receiver was trembling.

"We need five thousand euros and fast!" he blurted out the moment Spiegeltent said hello.

He carried on to explain about their encounter with the Kuchkins.

"Yes, it looks like those Russians are not going to budge, "Spiegeltent mused aloud. "This means our whole experiment is under threat."

"But this is awful!" fumed Viktor. "Isn't there anything at all we can do? How about your research money?"

"We have been using them for flights, accommodation and other expenses and now only have a couple of thousand euros left," the Professor replied. He could not tell Viktor that the sum in question now had to cover the Cs' trip to Majorca as well as the Ks', so there was practically nothing of it left.

"So what are we going to do?"

"Well, I have an idea which may work," Spiegeltent said enigmatically. "But it will take me a couple of hours to find out. Why don't you wait in the hotel bar? It is open all night and has sofas, so you can make your wife comfortable while you wait. I will call you to say whether my little plan has worked or not, so don't switch off your phone."

The Professor disconnected the call and went out of the hotel building, but instead of getting into his hired car, parked nearby, he flagged down a passing Blue cab and told the driver to take him to the *Casino de Mallorca*. He didn't have time to try and find it himself.

"I am sorry, but on Professor Spiegeltent's instructions, we have to part company here and now," Superintendent Burgess, looking tired and sombre, announced to Catherine and Victor.

The local time was 3.30 am. They had just landed in Palma and were waiting for their luggage to come off the conveyor belt in the semi-empty arrivals lounge.

"But what are we supposed to do?" asked Catherine.

"That depends on what you were doing on your previous visit here," Burgess shrugged. "With Dan... sorry, Professor Spiegeltent, we have decided that, in your case, we could safely skip the Pollenca bit of your journey. What exactly did you do on arrival in Palma by an early morning coach?"

"Well, it was still very early, and we had the whole day to kill before our late-afternoon return flight, so from the coach station we took a taxi to the airport to drop our suitcases in the left luggage office there," said Victor.

"What time was that?"

"About 6 am, I think."

"And then? Please be as precise as you can."

"And then, after a quick and very uncomfortable snooze in the airport's arrivals lounge, we took a taxi straight to a beach in Iletas, near Magaluf."

"Yes, we thought it would be nice to spend our last hours in Majorca on a beach before catching the flight back home," Catherine added.

"Well, that's precisely what you are going to do now," said Burgess. "Deposit your bags to the left luggage office, then hang on here until 8 am, like last time, and go straight to the beach.

"How about you?" Victor asked.

"Don't worry about me. True, I must get out of the picture now, but rest assured: I will be keeping a good eye on you and will always be there to help in case of emergency. Also, if you desperately need my advice, do not hesitate to call. But otherwise, you have to be on your own, just as you were on your previous visit. This is extremely important, if you were to cherish even the slightest hope of returning to where you came from. So if by accident you get a glimpse of the Ks, or anyone else you know from afar – run away from them!"

Burgess grinned and, having handed to the Petrovs a brand-new mobile phone, scribbled down his number on the margins of Victor's boarding pass.

"Don't lose it!" he said and, having picked up his travel bag from the conveyor belt, walked away resolutely.

Having left the airport building, he flagged down a Blu Cab Company blue-light taxi and flashed his police badge in the face of the driver:

"Could you please drive somewhere, from where I could have a good view of the terminal's exit without being seen myself, then stop and wait for my further instructions?"

The driver turned the ignition key and nodded: "*Si, senor!* Yes, sir."

He pulled over in an abandoned parking bay around the corner, from where the taxi rank could be clearly seen.

"Perfect!" said Burgess. "Now, let's wait and see."

"I find him arrogant and somewhat dumb, that policeman of ours," said Victor. With their cabin bags and two in-hold suitcases they had just picked up, the Petrovs were sitting on a hard and uncomfortable bench in the arrivals lounge.

"I think you are simply jealous, Vitya. He is a straightforward no-nonsense man, who knows what he is doing," said Catherine. "And don't worry: I do not fancy him at all."

"Unlike our friend Viktor K," Victor C noted sarcastically.

"Well, I have to confess I do find him attractive, but only because he reminds me of you, silly. A slightly perfected version of yourself, so to speak…"

"I feel the same about Katherine K," Victor sighed. "Listen, don't you think we could put aside all those bans and try to find them?"

"Don't be so ridiculous, Vitya, and try to contain your lust. We are about to get our only minuscule chance of getting back home, and you are ready and willing to ruin it all before it even starts for the sake of one quick snog with a near-stranger!"

"Yes, Catia, but isn't that what love is about? Don't get me wrong: I do love YOU to bits. But I feel that I love her too for being exactly like you and still a tad different."

"Oh, well, thanks for being honest at least. When will this whole nightmare end, I wonder?"

The Petrovs went silent and Catherine tried to nod off, having put her head on her husband's chest.

Victor suddenly pushed his wife's head to the side and jumped up from the bench.

"We forgot!" he shouted.

"What? What did we forget?" Catherine panicked.

"We forgot to deposit our bags to the left luggage room, like we did before!"

"But is it that important?"

"Don't you remember what Professor Spiegeltent said? Every little detail is of extreme importance if we want to activate the law of probabilities!"

"Let's do it now," said Catherine. "What a day."

She got off the bench, yawned, stretched and, having made sure the plaster sticker was still on her forehead by touching it gently, began pulling her suitcase towards the left luggage office. Victor followed her.

Twenty minutes later, the Cs were back on the arrivals lounge bench. They still had a couple of hours to rest before they were scheduled to take a cab to the Magaluf beach where Victor would have to try and re-enact his jellyfish sting. From *Majorca Bulletin*, a local English-language newspaper which he picked in a 24/7 Relay shop in the lounge, he learned that jellyfish were still in abundance in Majorcan coastal waters, so irritating one to the point when it would sting him again should not be that hard, or so he thought. He only hoped the sting would not be too painful this time.

Having left the Cs dozing on the hard airport bench, let's now return to the Ks whom, unlike the Petrovs, we do not have to avoid.

It's been nearly three hours since they – with Olga's permission – installed themselves in the corner of the vast BonSol bar. Katherine, exhausted after another bout of vomiting, was dozing on a couchette, with Viktor sitting awkwardly at her feet nursing a warm *pina colada*. He felt frustrated and fed up. With Katherine, with himself, with the world where they were trapped at the moment and from where they were trying to escape, with the universe they, allegedly, had come from and with all other alternative worlds and universes in existence.

"There is no way Spiegeltent will be able to get five grand in Majorca in the middle of the night," he was thinking bitterly. "He may be a professor alright, but not a bank robber."

At that very moment, his phone rang.

"I've got the lot and must pass it on to you immediately!" Spiegeltent's triumphant voice was trembling with excitement. "Are you in the bar? I will be with you in ten minutes, but not to disrupt the flow of probabilities completely, will only spend two or three minutes with you. On your last visit, you were asleep at this time of the night – I've checked with your notes – so any potential damage our quick meeting can do to the schedule of the experiment should be minimal."

Dishevelled and ruddy-faced, the Professor barged into the bar ten minutes later and headed for the solitary patron, who was Viktor.

"Don't wake her up," he said on spotting Katherine supine on the sofa. He then looked at his watch.

"We only have three minutes to talk, Viktor, so let's be quick."

Only now Viktor noticed that Spiegeltent was holding a tattered plastic bag with semi-visible words *Casino de Mallorca* on it.

He threw the bag on the table, then picked it up, turned it upside down – and...

Hundreds of rumpled and not very clean banknotes fell out and began pirouetting above the table. Some of them landed on the floor.

Viktor looked stunned.

"How... where... did you get them?" he muttered.

"It's too long a story. Will tell you some other time. Remember: we only have three minutes. Just pick them up and take the lot to the Kuchkins pronto! Wake them up, let the bastards suffer a little!" he told Viktor with uncharacteristic spite in his normally well-balanced professorial voice.

Viktor's reaction was unexpected.

"I can't do this, Professor!" he said. "I can't take the money until you tell me how you've managed to procure such a large sum in less than two hours. I hardly know you, after all. You claim to be a professor, and you do talk smoothly. But, for all I know, you could also be an international criminal and a bank robber. And I'd much rather stay in this semi-literate universe forever than deal with dirty money. I am sure my wife would agree with me too," he pointed at Katherine snoring gently at his side.

It was clear to Spiegeltent that Viktor would not budge until he told him the truth.

"Alright, alright, young man," he said. "I will add a couple of minutes to this impromptu and highly undesirable, from the Probability Theory angle, encounter of ours. Let me assure you first of all that I am not a criminal or a bank robber. Do you think Superintendent Burgess would call me his best friend, had I been a rogue? I don't think so."

Viktor shrugged and had a sip of his lukewarm *pina colada.*

"Nor am I a gambler," Spiegeltent continued. "But I am a mathematician and one of this world's top experts in the Theory of Probability and the Probability Perspective. To illustrate them, in my university lectures and scientific papers, I often use the example of a casino. It is a well-known fact that casinos always win over the punters in the end, and this is really so, for otherwise the former would not have been able to sustain themselves. The key words here are 'in the end', or 'eventually', if you wish, because in reality a gambler can keep winning for a period of time. If at that point, he stops and leaves the casino, he would be in profit. The problem with inveterate gamblers is that they never leave until they lose all their money which happens inevitably as long as they carry on playing indefinitely."

"This is all obvious," commented Viktor. "Could you please stop beating about the bush and explain how you won all that money."

"I'll try to make it as brief and as simple as possible," Spiegeltent felt in his element again. He stood up. Pacing around the bar table, at which Viktor was sitting, he began speaking in an excited and rather loud voice. Luckily, except for the two, or rather three of them, if we remember Katherine who was still dozing fitfully on the sofa, there was no one else in the bar at this late, or rather early, hour.

"I was hoping the casino where I went would have a roulette table, and it did. I have always experienced a kind of perverse fascination with roulette – not only as a mathematician, but also as an avid reader of literature. Remember Tolstoyevsky's *The Gambler*. 'The roulette wheel has no memory and no conscience'. Well, the roulette wheel may indeed not possess much in terms of conscience or memory, but – like everything else in the universe – it is still susceptible to the Calculus of Probabilities, one of our world's main non-religious scriptures, so to speak. I can even say that it can serve as one of the Probability Law's most graphic real-life illustrations. Now, there are all kinds of bets you can do on the roulette: on the odd numbers, on black, on red, on even numbers, and so on. No matter which bet you go for, there will always be eighteen spots on which you can win and twenty spots on which you lose, so on average, if you bet, say, 100 euros, you will routinely lose nearly five and a half euros on each bet. This doesn't look too good, does it? But luckily, there are other types of roulette bets too. There are the so-called 'dozens' where you bet on a random selection of twelve different numbers, and there's a good chance that the odds will initially be in your favour. Again, I stress 'initially' here, for eventually, if you do not stop on time, you are going to lose!"

In his excitement, Spiegeltent mechanically, without thinking, picked up Viktor's cocktail from the table, took a big sip and put it back down.

"But what if you chose to bet on just one single number, which is allowed too?" he continued. "If, for example, you put ten euros on, say, number eleven, then, if the wheel eventually stops at eleven, you win 350 euros, and if it doesn't, you lose just ten! You can then keep betting for a while, and at the point when you come out ahead and win a substantial sum, as I did, you have to resolutely say 'no' to further stakes and, having collected your money, leave the building, before the casino staff finds a way to keep you there for a bit longer, i.e. until you lose it all: they have a whole list of very clever ruses to that effect, I can assure you!"

"From what you said, Professor, it appears that anyone who follows your pattern can repeat your actions and win," Victor objected meekly.

"Well, young man, I haven't told you the full story of course. To properly calculate my moves, I had to use deductive logic and a lot of pure mathematics which I wouldn't want to bore you with. But the main factor – and I want you to remember this very well, my friend – was pure old luck! Yes, the result could have easily been disappointing, but I was in luck tonight, just like, it seems, all of us, including that disgusting couple, the Kuchkins!"

Viktor was already on his knees picking up the banknotes from the floor.

"They should blacklist you in all the casinos of the universe," he muttered to the Professor jokingly.

"They certainly will as of this morning," Spiegeltent smiled. "But now, not to test the probabilities law even further, I'd better leave you. Hope you enjoy your old room."

He ran out of the hotel into the sticky subtropical night, jumped into his hired car and drove off.

Chapter Nineteen

Sequences of the Consequences

It was early morning. The sun had just risen from behind the mountains, and the touch of its first morning rays on Catherine's hand, sticking out the cab window, felt gentle and almost intimate. The road to Magaluf ran past countless olive groves, surrounded by hills, meadows and terraced vineyards, all basking in the warm water-colour-ish light of the sunrise.

"Wherever we may be and whatever this world is called, it is beautiful," Catherine was thinking. She looked at her husband, dozing next to her, his head on her shoulder. Catherine was pleased that Victor was resting before his approaching swim among the jellyfish, which promised to be stressful and nerve-racking.

Inside the taxi a couple of hundred yards behind them, Superintendent Burgess covered his mouth with his hand to suppress a powerful yawn. He hadn't had a proper sleep for over twenty-four hours and was literally dying for a quick nap.

"Listen, mate," he said to the driver. "I am going to have a quick shut-eye now, but please keep following that Blu Cab in front of us. I know they are going to a beach in Magaluf, so please wake me up as we approach it."

"*Si, Senor!*" said the driver. "*Duerma bien!* Sleep well!"

Bekki Beach in Magaluf was nearly empty at this early hour, apart from a handful of early-morning bathers, mostly Germans, flocking together near the sea edge and talking loudly pointing at something in the water.

"See, they are reluctant to get into the sea because of the jellyfish," Catherine noted. "There must be plenty of them this morning, so we are in luck."

"Speak for yourself," Victor said grimly. "I don't consider the prospect of getting another sting particularly lucky."

"You are my hero," Catherine said warmly, with only a slight touch of sarcasm, and patted her husband on the head.

"It all looks the same as a week ago," said Victor, somewhat appeased by his wife's gesture. "I think last time we came to the beach a couple of hours later though."

Catherine consulted her notes.

"Yes, you are right, Vitya. We have nearly two hours to kill. Why don't you commandeer a couple of sun loungers from that man in the shed? We both could do with another snooze, I reckon."

Victor took off his sandals and trundled off towards the shed. On his way, he nearly bumped into Burgess, who left his shelter behind the bushes to hire a lounger too. The policeman, sleepy as he was, spotted Victor in time to quickly back down and disappear from view.

The first thing Katherine did on entering room 25 after the Kuchkins' hasty (and happy, for they could not believe their luck: to have earned five grand without – literally – lifting their ample bottoms off the bed) departure was to vomit into the bathroom sink.

"The room has been initiated now. Just like last time," Victor commented dryly. He then looked at his watch ."And, according to our schedule, almost on the dot too."

"Stop making fun of me, Vitya," Katherine said, breathing heavily. "Don't forget it was by sheer coincidence that I got the poisoning and not you."

The Kuchkins had left the room in total disarray. Wine corks were scattered all over the floor; cushions and blankets were piled in the middle of a capacious queen-size double bed the size of a medieval town square.

"Just like last time, you'll have to sleep in it on your own," Katherine said, pointing at the bed. "So you'd better tidy it up. As for me – just like last time – I will feel more comfortable on the sofa."

"That's a shame, darling," Viktor smiled. "I think sleeping in this enormous bed on one's own should be classified as a minor offence. Or a breach of public order."

"Not funny, Vitya. Besides, you cracked precisely the same joke a week ago, remember?"

"But, Katia, I am doing this deliberately!" Viktor lied. "Remember what Professor Spiegeltent said: every movement from our last visit, no matter how small and insignificant it may seem, needs to be repeated, if we are to stand even the slightest chance of success. So, now, after we finish unpacking, we'll call the cleaners to tidy the room up while we walk downstairs for breakfast. Or, wait, I think we actually had breakfast at an *al fresco* restaurant on the beach. You said you needed fresh air, but still vomited all over the table there. An encore is now required!"

"Well, this time I do not want any breakfast at all – inside or *al fresco*. I think I feel much worse than I did last time."

"I know it must be hard, Katia. But you are a brave woman. Remember what you and Catherine did to those bullies in the Camford pub? I was so proud of you two then."

"Stop patronising me, Vitya. It was your job to protect us. Not ours."

"Let's not argue and try to stick to the schedule, which means going for breakfast together. You will have a chance to rest afterwards," Viktor said in reconciliation.

"That's all we do. We argue." Katherine whispered to herself and went back to the bathroom to apply some make up to her uncharacteristically pale and swollen face.

"What time is it?" Victor asked Catherine sleepily.

Wearing nothing but swimsuits, there were lying on two sun loungers next to each other. The mercilessly hot and bright Majorcan sun was already fairly high up in the sky and was shining above Bekki Beach for all it was worth.

With her eyes semi-closed, Catherine threw a furtive look at her watch.

"Gosh, it's past ten o'clock," she said. "Time to go for a swim, Vitya."

"I know," Victor sighed and got up. "Wish us luck. I mean myself and the jellyfish."

"You'll both be ok, I am sure. Don't swim too far behind the buoy and don't tease the poor creature too much. Make sure you head back for the shore the moment you get stung. I will have the towel and the ointment ready. Just like last time, my medical training should come handy."

Catherine reached into her bag and took out a small bottle of antiseptic cream they bought in a pharmacy last time.

"Hide it!" Victor said angrily. "This ointment is no good, don't you understand? We have to go back to the same pharmacy and buy it again!"

"Of course. How could I forget? Never mind, Vitya. Don't get stressed before the swim. *Ni pukha, ni pera...* Neither fluff nor feather!" said Catherine using Victor's favourite Russian idiomatic expression meaning "best of luck to you". What fluff and feather had to do with good fortune was a mystery to her. And Victor himself, despite being a journalist and hence a sort of a man of letters, had never been able to explain it to her.

While still on the beach, Viktor could see a couple of semi-transparent, or rather semi-opaque, round creatures, their brown tentacles stirring in the warm and shallow sea water. They were probably dead, he thought, but walked into the water carefully trying not to step on any of them.

He trudged through the water – away from the beach – past groups of bathers, mostly children, splashing in shallow places near the shore, until there were no other swimmers in sight. The sea was alluringly aquamarine and pleasantly warm. Closely watched by

Catherine from the beach and, unbeknownst to him, by Burgess from behind the bushes, Victor – a strong and confident swimmer ever since his Russian childhood – took a deep breath and dived in. Having re-emerged, he briskly swam ahead free-style trying not to think about jellyfish or any other sea creatures down there until he reached the bright-orange buoy.

Having grabbed the rough slippery cable underneath the buoy, Victor stopped to regain his breath and looked back at the shore. He could see his wife in a red bikini, no more than a red dot from where he was. Just as on the previous occasion, he waved to her and could discern the dot waving back.

It was time to search for jellyfish. Victor knew they would normally be sitting under the buoy – that was how he was stung last time, by sticking his hand underneath it.

He was about to repeat his manoeuvre and instinctively looked down at the sea water under the buoy. To his horror, he saw a long – very long – moving shadow straight under his bobbing feet. The next moment he felt a brush of rough cold skin against his back and then a sharp burning pain in his right hand, arm and shoulder. The water around him was quickly turning pink. He realised with sudden clarity that whatever had bitten him was not a jellyfish…

"Excuse us, but can my wife and I join you?"

A pleasantly suave elderly gentlemen in a panama hat was bending above Viktor and Katherine's table at the *al fresco* beach restaurant where the Ks were about to have breakfast. The two seats at their table were the only remaining vacant ones.

Both Viktor and Katherine knew that their breakfast had to culminate with Katherine vomiting all over the table, like she did on the previous occasion. That in itself was not difficult to arrange: Katherine felt sick enough to be ready to throw up any time. But how about the elderly couple who wanted to sit next to them? Wasn't it Viktor's duty to forewarn them of the impending danger?

"Well... well... I am not so sure," he mumbled semi-coherently, looking down at his plate, piled with scrambled eggs on two large slices of brown toast. "You... you are welcome of course, but... you should know that my wife is not very well... and is prone to... vomiting... so you may end up being... er... disappointed... sorry..."

"This young lady?" the man enquired incredulously "She doesn't look at all sick to me... What do you think, darling?"

His last question was addressed to his wife – a graceful and stylish old lady, wearing a tight cardigan on top of her loose sarafan-style beach dress, despite the very warm weather. She was standing next to her husband with a loaded tray in her hands.

It was Katherine's turn to intervene.

"You don't believe I am sick?" she said with a grin. "Well, here's the proof!"

A stream of vomit burst out of her mouth, just missing the old lady's sarafan.

Mumbling some incoherent excuses under their breath, the elderly couple hastily retreated.

"Job done! We can safely tick another box!" Viktor said looking down at the puddle of vomit on the table with satisfaction and delight, as if it was a piece of his favourite Napoleon cake about to be devoured. "Let's go back to our room, darling. You need some rest now."

...Victor gave out a piercing yell. "Shark! Shark! Help me please!"

The upper part of his body felt paralysed, and he was unable to swim. The only way he could still keep himself above the surface was by moving his feet frantically and thus drawing the beast's attention to himself again.

He could hear piercing screams from the distance as all the swimmers who were still in the sea rushed back towards the shore. Parents were snatching their children out of the water and running away from the beach fast.

Catherine, scared out of her mind, ran towards the sea, fully determined to jump in and to swim to the buoy to save her husband. As she was about to run into the water, she was suddenly pushed aside by a tall bulky man.

"Don't you dare! Just stay where you are!" he shouted in the loud peremptory voice of a person used to giving commands and to being obeyed immediately.

It was Superintendent Burgess.

"Stay here and call an ambulance! And, for God's sake, a lifeboat, if there is one!" he shouted.

He ran into the sea and – with wide and resolute strokes – swam towards Victor, who, semi-conscious with pain and fear, kept clutching the buoy with both hands, as if clinging desperately to life itself.

He didn't know then that – in defiance of all probability laws – he had become victim to something extremely rare in Majorcan waters: a blue shark attack. There had only been eight shark sightings off the island during the previous twenty years, and just one other attack – on a hapless surfer who got away with a couple of scratches. Later, after the creature was caught, it transpired that it was probably a stray or a wounded blue shark which had got lost and ended up so close to the shore while chasing its prey. Whatever the prey was, the shark must have caught up with it, for – luckily for Victor – it was not terribly hungry and, after biting his arm, was not in hurry to attack again – just circled underneath thinking (if sharks can think) about what to do next.

It would have probably swum away, had it not been for some more severe turbulence above its long rounded snout – super-sensitive and full of extra-sharp teeth.

The turbulence was caused by Superintendent Burgess who, having reached the buoy, grabbed Victor under the armpits. "Hold on to me!" he yelled.

Then something extraordinary happened. The shark, disturbed by the splashes and by the sound of Burgess's very loud voice, grabbed the policeman by the feet and dragged him underwater.

With horror, Victor watched the Superintendent's head suddenly take a dive and disappear, never to be seen again.

"A-aa!" he screamed at the top of his lungs.

A lifeboat called by Catherine was approaching quickly. In a second or two, pairs of strong lifeguards' hands lifted Victor out of the sea and dragged him up on board.

"Where is the policeman? Where is he? The shark took him!" Victor kept shouting.

The lifeguards looked around, then took out their binoculars and scrutinised the sea as far as the horizon, but could see neither the shark nor Superintendent Burgess. The sea around the buoy and as far as one could see was quiet, as if nothing at all had just happened there. After a minute or so, the boat turned around and sped towards the shore.

Chapter Twenty

Consequences of the Sequences

Inside the ambulance taking the Cs to Son Espases hospital, Victor was spread on a stretcher. His wound was not deep and did not seem life-threatening, but he was in shock.

Catherine sat next to him holding his other, unbitten, hand.

"It's… it's the same spot…" Victor muttered semi-audibly, as if in delirium, as the ambulance, its sirens on, dashed along the motorway.

"What are you talking about, darling? Which spot?" asked Catherine worriedly.

"The shark's bite is in exactly the same spot where the jellyfish sting was… Not too much deviation… Don't think it would matter much for the probabilities rules which creature it was that bit me… Good for our mission…" Victor kept blabbering.

"Don't you worry about the mission or anything, Vitya! The main thing now is to get you to the hospital in time to disinfect the wound and prevent sepsis!"

"No, Katia, I want to continue with our experiment," Victor insisted. "This is what the poor policeman died for."

"You don't know: he may still be alive," said Catherine.

"I don't think so. You should have seen the beast that took him… What a horrible way to go! It could have been me, you know."

Victor was right. Superintendent Burgess did not survive the attack. His mutilated body was washed ashore later that afternoon, shortly after the shark was spotted, harpooned and killed by the lifeguards about half a mile away from the shore.

Professor Spiegeltent found out about his friend's death from the *Majorca Bulletin* the following morning. His immediate impulse was to abort the experiment and return home.

But that was just a momentary weakness on his part.

"Peter would want us to carry on," he was thinking while sitting in his car outside BonSol Hotel and waiting for the Ks to emerge. "Besides, if we prove beyond doubt that both couples did come from alternative universes, as I am sure they did, it would mean that the Many Worlds Interpretation of quantum mechanics is right and therefore different versions of Peter Burgess may still be alive and carrying out their policeman's or other duties elsewhere – in countless other universes."

The thought calmed him down considerably. Again, he felt like a true scientific pioneer pursuing his noble goal despite the terribly adverse circumstances, the death of his old colleague and friend – all for the benefit of humankind.

Spiegeltent decided not to break the news to the Ks, hoping they wouldn't be reading local newspapers or watching TV – which they didn't. The Petroffs only had two more days to go before their return flight to the UK, the flight during which, as Spiegeltent had reason to believe, they could be teleported back to the very dimension they had originally come from. As for the Cs, who arrived later and therefore had to stay on in Majorca for a day longer than the Ks, he had to reassure them as much as he could and persuade them to carry on with the mission.

He took out his mobile and dialled Victor's number.

The Petrovs were resting in a small room of their budget Horizonte Hotel – the same room they had stayed in on their previous visit (unlike the Ks, they were in luck: the room was vacant) when Victor's phone rang. He had been discharged from Son Espases a couple of hours after admission the day before. They disinfected Victor's wound, which proved insignificant, fed him a handful of strong painkillers and let him go. On the way to their hotel, Victor insisted on pulling over near the same pharmacy where they bought the ointment a week or so ago. He asked Catherine to go in and buy it again, despite the fact that an anti-jellyfish-sting balm was unlikely to be of much help in treating a shark bite.

Catherine's initial reaction to all those happenings was similar to that of Spiegeltent: she wanted to stop their quest and fly back to the UK immediately. But Victor managed to persuade her to keep going. "This is our only chance to get back home," he said. "We only have three days left to go. Besides, if we stop now, it would appear as if the policeman died and I got wounded all for nothing!" Reluctantly, his wife agreed to carry on.

The phone kept ringing and Victor picked it up.

"Hallo!"

"This is Daniel Spiegeltent calling. Is it a good time to talk?"

"Sure", said Victor and added: "I am sorry about your loss. I know you were old friends with Mr Burgess."

"Yes, it is a horrible blow, from which I will probably never recover," Spiegeltent sighed. "Peter... Superintendent Burgess was a remarkable man: capable, bright and compassionate in equal measure. I heard he was the only person on the beach who actually tried to save you."

"Yes, I'll never forget him," Victor whispered.

"Well, the fond memory of Peter makes it a moral duty for us to bring our experiment, in which he was so much involved, to its conclusion, wouldn't you agree?"

"Yes, sir," Victor nodded in agreement as if Professor Spiegeltent was next to him in the room and could appreciate his nods.

"The problem is that you and your lovely wife are now left without a supervisor to assist you in an emergency. I will have to keep chaperoning your... er... opposite numbers, who are still here too. They only have two days left in Majorca and will be flying back to the UK on Friday afternoon."

Having said that, the Professor immediately regretted it. He was not supposed to spill out to the Cs any information about the Ks' movements and vice versa, in case they decided to break the rules and meet up. "I am not a policeman, like Peter, who would have never made such a boo-boo," he thought ruefully, hoping against hope that Victor would not register that particular bit of information. Judging by Victor's next question, the Professor's guess was correct.

"And when are WE leaving?" Victor asked.

"I've booked you on an early morning flight the following day, the same flight you took initially. In the meantime, please keep sticking as much as possible to your previous visit's routine. You know that anyway. Busy as I am overseeing the Ks, I will try and keep an eye on you too. And hope your hand heals fast."

"Thank you, Professor," said Victor. "Commiserations again on your friend's death."

"Well," he said to his wife, having disconnected the call. "What's on our itinerary for today? I think I can guess. But you know what, probability or not, I am not setting foot on that beach ever again!"

The next couple of days were uneventful. Just as on the previous occasion, both Katherine and Victor were recovering from their respective ailments (food poisoning and a shark bite) quickly. As for Viktor, he had been feeling inexplicable dull pain in his right hand for a couple of days until it suddenly disappeared.

Professor Spiegeltent, having made sure his friend's body was ready to be flown to the UK for burial the following week, was falling over backwards to try and keep an eye on both couples, making sure their paths never crossed. The Cs and the Ks were attending different beaches, having meals in different restaurants and even watching different programmes on tellies in their respective rooms – all in accordance with their previous visits' schedules. Professor Spiegeltent was tempted to conclude that, forgetting for a moment Superintendent Burgess's horrific death and Victor's psychological trauma caused by the shark attack, the experiment was progressing well, thus increasing the chances for a happy resolution which meant safe return to their respective universes for both couples and (who knows) a possible Bonel Prize nomination for himself.

On Friday, at about midday, Spiegeltent called Viktor, instructing him and his wife to check out of the hotel and head for the airport, where they were to pick up their tickets for flight J59 to Stansted.

"Won't you come to the airport to say goodbye?" Viktor asked him.

"I'd love to but I can't, and you know why. But I may see you soon back in the UK. In case our experiment fails of course which I hope is not going to happen. So, if I never see you again, thanks for everything and have a good life back in your universe!"

Spiegeltent duly followed the Ks to the airport, made sure they picked up their tickets and went through immigration control. He could not proceed any further and decided to have a quick drink in the arrivals lounge bar before heading back to the city and finding a quiet spot near or inside Horizonte Hotel, from where he could keep an eye on the Cs until their departure the following morning, by which time he would already know whether the Ks had succeeded or not.

As the Professor was sipping his drink in the arrivals lounge, Victor and Catherine were in a Blu Cab taxi taking them to the airport.

Sure enough, the piece of information about the Ks's departure, so carelessly spilled out by Spiegeltent, did not fly past Victor's ears unrecorded. After a number of subsequent discussions with Catherine, the Petrovs decided that it could be their last chance ever to see the Ks and as such they simply could not miss it.

"Why can't we all take that flight together and see what happens?" Catherine was saying to her husband excitedly.

"You know what: I tend to agree with you here," he replied. "Just like being bitten by a shark instead of a jellyfish should not upset the apple cart of the experiment, or so I hope, flying out of here several hours earlier shouldn't either. The main thing is not to bump into Spiegeltent on the way."

But they nearly did.

As they were getting out of the cab, the Professor was leaving the airport building – looking around and blinking myopically in search of his parked car – no more than fifty yards away from the Cs, who, on seeing him, ducked and hid behind a white mini-van.

They were saved by a large group of young people carrying banners saying "Tourism Kills Majorca!" and throwing confetti at the airport crowd. They were members of Arran, an extremist anti-tourism youth organisation, who had come to the airport to demonstrate. At times, to the protesters' own delight, the media referred to them as anti-tourism terrorists, although their peaceful 'terrorism' was limited to throwing confetti and smashing a couple of restaurant and shop windows. Yet, on this occasion, their sudden appearance between the Cs and Professor Spiegeltent saved the former from being spotted.

In any case, the Professor's eyesight left much to be desired, and he never noticed the Petrovs, who, having bent as low as they could over a luggage trolley and trying to mix as much as possible with the noisy crowd of anti-tourism demonstrators, ran towards the airport building.

They were lucky at the ticket window: there were just two last seats left on flight J59 due to take off in half an hour. The money left from Superintendent Burgess' allowance was just enough to pay for them.

It would have been too late to check-in the bags. Luckily, this time the Cs only had cabin baggage, so they proceeded straight to immigration, then to customs. In no time, they ran inside the departure lounge, from where the flight had just started boarding.

"Katherine! Viktor! We are here!" they shouted.

An amazing scene followed. The few passengers who were still in the lounge could see two couples of twins, having dropped their bags and suitcases, hugging and kissing passionately, as if they hadn't seen each other for donkey's years.

As the final call was announced through a loudspeaker by a uniformed flight attendant, all four of them – holding hands and smiling happily – proceeded to board.

Epilogue

It all came – quite literally – out of the blue and cloudless sky behind the plane windows.

"Ladies and gentlemen, please fasten your seat belts: we are entering an area of slight turbulence!"

The voice of the captain on the intercom was cheerful, almost triumphant – as if he had just won a EuroMillions jackpot.

The Boeing was tossed about in the sky like a lump of ice in a cocktail mixing glass of that mighty bartender called God. Some bags and suitcases fell out of overhead lockers, which sprang open like flick-knife blades, and down onto the passengers' heads. Women were screaming...

Then it all suddenly stopped. The plane straightened up its course, and was floating smoothly through the deep-blue sky, interspersed with occasional tiny clouds.

It was soon time to strap in for landing. The captain duly apologised for the earlier turbulence, as if it was indeed his fault.

A man and woman, both in their late thirties or early forties and both just off Flight J59 from Palma, were propelled into the arrivals hall amid the throng of disembarking passengers.

They stopped at immigration control, took out their passports, and for the first time, it seemed, had a chance to look properly at each other. After a minute or so, they fell into each other's arms with obvious relief. Yet something made them hesitate before kissing, and they drew apart again staring at each other, suddenly uncertain.

"Does your name start with a K or a C?" asked the man nervously.

She looked doubtful.

"I'm not telling you how I spell my name. Not just yet... Maybe, I am not sure myself... Why don't we get out of here and go home?"

The man smiled. "Nice idea. Whatever the spelling, I think you're very lovely."

'Well, that's a good start," she said.

They walked through the crowded arrivals hall to the baggage reclaim area hand in hand.

"I cannot help the feeling that I am not the man I used to be," he said.

It was now her turn to smile. "No," she said. "Perhaps you're not."

A red police car was parked right next to the terminal's exit.

"**POLEESE"** was written on its roof and sides in large letters.

The man squinted at the car.

"I think we are being met," he said to the woman.

Inside, Superintendent Peter Burgess was grinning at them from behind the wheel.

2015 – 2017

Hertfordshire – Majorca – Budapest

About the Author

Vitali Vitaliev was born in 1954 in Kharkiv, Ukraine. He first made a name for himself in the then Soviet Union, writing satirical journalism in *Krokodil* and other publications, exposing the activies of organised crime and the all-permeating corruption in the collapsing country. His fearless stance ultimately led to his defection in 1990.

He has appeared regularly on TV and radio in the UK (*Have I Got News For You, Saturday Night Clive, Today, Start the Week*), was a writer/researcher for *QI* and has contributed to newspapers and magazines all over the world.

He is the author of thirteen books, written in English and translated into a number of foreign languages, including German, Japanese, Russian, Finnish and Italian.

Vitali now lives in Herfordshire.

"Vitaliev has a sharp and sardonic eye; and his observations are informed by his humanity and compassion." *Daily Telegraph*

"Vitali Vitaliev is a star in the making."
Time magazine

"Vitaliev has an irrepressible sense of humour"
The *Guardian*

Also by Vitali Vitaliev

Granny Yaga
A fantasy novel for Children and Adults

"Granny Yaga follows the switchback adventures of a boy called Danny, growing up in North London where the local she-dragons are notorious fighters, and any alert passer-by can spot Granny herself flying low over the British Museum. Danny becomes Granny's aide-de-camp in a life-or-death duel with the demon Koschei, fought out in the London underground, in disused stations, boarded-up houses and the enchanted skies over Crouch End, with back-up from the relatively orthodox magic of Yesterdayland (huts on chicken legs, talking cats, self-catering tablecloths) and the realpolitik of its neighbouring Soviet satellite, a land of cruel edicts and capricious tsars where the workers and permanently drunk, and the loo seats belonging to each family in a communal flat hang side by side on the wall 'like luckless horseshoes'. A gripping read for all ages, from Danny's to Granny's." Hilary Spurling

"Granny Yaga is for the child in a grown-up and the grown-up in a child… The reader flies along with the narrative, never feeling like getting off, hoping the journey will never end and feeling sad that, like all superb books, it has to." Alexander Boot, author, columnist and blogger

"Delightfully inventive. Wickedly funny." Marina Lewycka, author of A Short History of Tractors in Ukranian

Printed in Great Britain
by Amazon